WHAT THE CRITICS ARE SAYING:

"...a great job in creating two characters so opposite from each other..." Lena C. for Fallen Angel Reviews

"Taming Tess is a funny take on The Taming of the Shrew. I will be adding Roxi Romano's *Taming Tess* to my keeper collection." Joyfully Reviewed

"Taming Tess is a story about what it takes for a man like Roman St. John to bring a woman like Tess Abbot to her senses and see that she can have it all if she'd only let go of her fears and inhibitions. ...a truly funny romantic comedy that will keep readers laughing throughout." Two Lips Reviews

4 ½ hearts "This is a well-written, humorous story that had me laughing out loud and I really enjoyed it as the sparks flew between these two lovable characters; I could not wait to see what they would get into next as I flew through the pages." Sandra for The Romance Studio

4 Stars "This is a fast-moving story with delightful characters. The give and take between the hero and heroine is fun, and the adjustments they make as their relationship develops are nicely plotted. These two characters leave you believing that they have a future together." By Susan Mobley for Romantic Times Book Reviews

Architect Tess Abbot's house catches fire during renovation and blames Contractor Roman St. John. A man of his word, Roman honors a boast Tess goaded him into making. If the job isn't done on time she can move into his house.

But sexual tension and close quarters confound her resistance to the one man who can reduce career-minded Tess to wifely status. To win her love, Roman must tame Tess…but not too much…to keep her forever, in this modern day *Taming of the Shrew* story?

OTHER BOOKS & STORIES
BY BARBARA RAFFIN

Finding Home: St. John Sibling Series, Book 2
The Mating Game
The Scarecrow & Ms. Moon (novella)
Jaded (short story)
The Sting of Love (short story)
The Visitor
Time Out of Mind
Wolfsong
The Indentured Heart (historical)

TAMING TESS

St. John Sibling Series: Book 1

Barbara Raffin

Copyright © 2013

Plain Wrapper Publishing

Cover Art/Design: Covers by Rogenna
http://www.sweettoheat.blogspot.com
All rights reserved.

This is a work of fiction. People and locations, even those with real names, have been fictionalized for the purposes of this story.

TAMING TESS

St. John Sibling Series: Book 1

Barbara Raffin

CHAPTER ONE

Lady, if I don't finish your remodeling job by the end of the week, you can move into my *house.*

The words Roman St. John had spoken only days ago to Tess Abbot ricocheted around his brain as he stared into the flames devouring the third story of her house, the construction project he'd been within hours of finishing before it caught on fire. Whatever had possessed him to make such a ridiculous boast to the woman?

From the curb behind him, his truck horn blared. He glared over his shoulder at his client who sat in his truck leaning on the horn. Six weeks of that woman's constant haranguing, that's what had goaded him into being stupid enough to gamble on the reliability of his crew and to propose the ridiculous, that she move into his house if he didn't get her job done on time.

Besides, it hadn't seemed such an outrageous boast at the time he'd made it. He had a reputation as a contractor who got his jobs done on schedule, even when the client was a pain in the behind control freak like Tess Abbot.

Now, here he was, less than twenty-four hours away from getting rid of the client from hell and his doofus cousin Raymond goes and sets fire to The Castle, by which the Victorian mansion of a house was known. If the man ever stuck another cigar in his mouth, Roman vowed to cram it down Raymond's throat, ash end first.

Honk. Honk. Hooonnnk.

And if his client didn't stop honking his truck horn in his ear, he was going to super glue her fingers to her harpy tongue. He stepped around to the driver's side of the truck and jerked open the door.

"What now?"

She squared her shoulders, folded her arms across her compact breasts flattened further by the tight weave of a skin-tight, spandex tank top, and lifted her pert chin to the imperial angle he'd come to know all too well in the weeks working for her. "I smell like the bottom of an ash tray. I want a bath and clearly my bathroom is no longer usable, thanks to your crew's carelessness."

"What do you want me to do about that?"

The strobe lights of the fire truck filling The Castle's driveway flashed through the evening dusk and across a face that was flawless save for a smudge of soot on one cheek and the flecks of ash salting her dark hair. A sweatband held her thick mane off her face and neck, as it always did during her daily runs. But, the day she'd opened her front door to him so he could begin renovations on The Castle, her hair had been a loose, bouncy bob reaching for her shoulders. Until that day, they'd communicated via phone calls, emails, and texts, her voice lush and inviting, her ideas and plans smart. Their conversations had had him thinking beyond an architect/contractor relationship. Given finding a wife and starting a family ranked at the top of his latest five-year plan, falling in love would have been an appropriate course of action. But…

"St. John. You do have a bathroom in your house, don't you?"

And there she went with another of her endless digs. Good thing he hadn't voiced his feelings the day they met, because six weeks of working with Tess had proven her to be anything but the type of woman with whom he wished to spend the rest of his life. The woman he'd come to know via phone had disappeared behind the one who kept looking over his shoulder—second guessing him and *always* there because she lived on the construction site.

Not that he didn't respect her point of view. She was a good architect, knew her stuff. But, even when a sub-contractor dismissed her opinion and he backed her up, had she appreciate his support? No. She'd curtly informed him she was capable of handling her own problems.

The red light washed across her face again, making him think less than charitable thoughts about his client. A crime, that's what it was for a woman to have a body that wouldn't quit and a tongue to match.

"Please let me put you up in a nice motel for the night," he said, hoping the woman had cooled off enough by now to realize the absurdity of moving into his house with him. They squabbled like cats and dogs.

"Your idea of *nice* no doubt rents by the hour in this town," she lobbed back at him.

And now another of the never-ending digs for the small community in which he'd chosen to build a business and raise a family. No doubt about it, she was two horns shy of a she-devil. There wasn't enough water in all the Great Lakes framing the state of Michigan to wash that fact away. He swung himself up into the driver's seat.

"Pine Mountain may be a small town in a forgotten corner of Michigan's Upper Peninsula," Roman said through his teeth, "but—"

"—It has clean air and quiet living," she

simpered back at him, "not to mention it's a great place to raise kids. Yada, yada, yada. Personally," she droned on, "I find quiet vastly overrated."

"Some quiet right now would be *vastly* refreshing," Roman grumbled, throwing the truck into gear.

"Look, St. John, I'm the one who's been burned out of her house with nothing more than the clothes on her back. And whose fault is that?"

Roman winced. Of all the people to have screwed up with, why did it have to be with the harpy from hell?

Then again he should be more tolerant of the woman since she'd come home from her evening run to find her house on fire—a fire for which he likely was responsible? He owed her more than a little compassion.

"Look," he tried one last time as he pulled away from the curb and edged around the backend of the fire truck that blocked Tess' car in her driveway. "We may not have any hotels in the area, but there are several Triple A motels."

"I'm used to five star accommodations."

The woman was unrelentingly stubborn. No wonder he couldn't help but spar with her at every turn. No wonder he'd dubbed her *Princess* by the end of the first week working with her.

Still, early evidence indicated he was responsible for her predicament. Maybe if he offered an olive branch of help, she'd be more reasonable.

"I know a clean-up crew I can get in here as soon as the Fire Chief clears the scene."

"You burn up so many of your projects you have a cleaning crew on stand-by?"

His fingers tightened on the steering wheel. "I

just happen to know them. They've got topnotch water extraction equipment."

"How nice of you to recommend *your* friends to clean up your mess. This is beginning to sound like a scam."

Okay. Trying to be a nice guy with Tess Abbot wasn't working. Time to try a different tact.

Turning hard from the side street onto the main thoroughfare, he said, "You'll accept nothing less than five star, huh?"

"That's right."

If the woman demanded five star accommodations, he was a free man. One look at his modest digs and she'd beg him to take her to a motel, any motel.

#

The minute they left the city limits, Tess should have demanded Roman St. John turn his truck around and take her back to town, but who could tell where city ended and country began? Not a Chicago bred girl like her, that's for sure. Even downtown Pine Mountain seemed sparsely lit in comparison.

Yet, here she was, driving into the descending gloom of nightfall with a man who was trouble with a capital T. All hunkness aside, Roman St. John and his *great place to raise kids* attitude sounded too much like her father, who still lived by the antiquated standards of a fifties' man. Daddy-Dearest believed women belonged in the bedroom not the boardroom.

She scowled, recalling the moment she'd realized her father had never intended for her to take over the family architectural firm. That the only way she would ever be recognized for her talent as an architect would be if she went out on her own.

And now the refurbishing job she'd intended to

use as the jewel in the foundation of her business was in flames. She no longer had a salable property ready to flip into the hands of a couple of potential high-end buyers-in-waiting let alone a photographable project for her portfolio. Her father would declare that she'd failed to go it on her own—the father who'd promoted lesser men ahead of her, *men* being the operative word. The father who'd refused to give her a recommendation to present to other architectural firms when she'd left his.

The father who'd informed every loan institution within a hundred mile radius of Chicago that they could not rely on him to underwrite any loan they gave the youngest of his three daughters. He'd probably even warned them that she, being a female, would undoubtedly default on the loan because he believed no woman could build a business on her own.

"You'll come crawling back to me before the year is out," he'd shouted after her as she'd stormed out of his office the day she'd finally realized the extent to which her father would go to keep her at heel.

Fortunately, she had great-aunt Honey to turn to. Aunt Honey had never let any man get in her way. Aunt Honey had been a career woman before it was fashionable and traveled her own flamboyant path in life undaunted by the naysayers.

Aunt Honey owned a house three hundred miles away from her father's influence—the kind of house whose renovation would be a shining star in any architect's portfolio. A smile tugged at the corner of Tess' mouth. Honey's reign as the grand dame of the local community players had lasted a decade and a half before the wanderlust had once again beckoned her. But fifteen years of summer visits had been long enough for Tess to learn an appreciation for fine old houses.

She'd bought The Castle from Aunt Honey at fair market value even though her aunt had offered it to her for less. It was the only fair thing to do since there'd been another buyer interested. Besides, anything less and her father would dismiss her success as having been subsidized by family.

She'd even gone the conventional route in financing the purchase rather than take Aunt Honey up on her offer of a land contract. A bank loan kept her independent, but it also meant she had to turn a profit before year's end when her balloon payment was due.

That end-of-year deadline is partly why she'd hired St. John, a contractor with a reputation for getting things done on time—a contractor known for his quality of workmanship and reliability. That and the fact Aunt Honey had recommended him. Between the tight timeline and Aunt Honey's high praise, she'd actually hired him sight unseen to renovate the Victorian era mansion. When she found out he was the other buyer she'd bought the place out from under—

"No hard feelings," he'd assured her. "I understand Honey selling to family."

It also meant he already knew the place well and that saved her a five hour drive from Chicago to show him the job. She faxed him her blueprints for the changes. They hammered out pre-job details via email, texting, and phone calls. That deep, assuring voice on the other end of the phone line had made her wonder far too much about the man it belonged to. She was still a woman with needs, after all, even if she weren't looking for happily-ever-after with any man.

And, when she'd opened the mansion's front door and looked into Roman St. John's chiseled-by-thirty-something years face, she knew he was everything his telephone voice had promised and more. Visions of a hot tryst danced in her head.

But, the first words out of Roman's mouth, once he'd determined she was indeed *the* Tess Abbot who'd hired him, took him down to the level of every man who'd ever doubted her.

"You're a lot younger than I expected."

"Don't let my looks fool you, Mr. St. John," she'd leveled back at him in her best authoritative tone when she'd wanted to shout out her frustration at looking even younger than her twenty-nine years. "I graduated top of my class and am a board certified architect in three states. Got those certifications on my first try at each test. I know what I'm doing."

"I didn't mean—"

She'd cut him off with a terse, "Of course you didn't."

Her opinion of him diminished further during their first walk-through when he'd lingered in the original nursery off the master bedroom which Honey had used as a dressing room and Tess slated to be converted to a state-of-the-art walk-in closet.

"A sweet little space," he'd said. "Convenient for a young couple starting a family."

"It's not like I'm removing the house's Victorian charm," she'd countered, readily defensive. "I'm just making an old fashioned nursery into a closet more functional for today's buyer. Besides, why are you so sentimental about it? If you'd gotten The Castle how else would you have made money off it than converted it to apartments?"

"Wasn't planning to make money off it," he'd said. "I was going to make The Castle into my family home."

His answer had slapped her in the face like a page out of her father's book. Only a family man would choose nursery over closet.

The phrase *barefoot and pregnant* burned between her ears. How many times had those words tumbled from her father's mouth on the kind of laugh he saved for his cronies? Never mind that her mother and sisters had custom closets full of designer heels. No barefooted for them. Then again they'd all played their domestic rolls perfectly in step with the old man, marrying and popping out babies. But not her. Subjugating herself to any man was not in her nature…or her future. Especially not after her father had betrayed her as he had.

That's why, no matter how much Roman St. John tweaked her hormones, she'd vowed the day of their first face-to-face meet there would be no flirting with him. Just business.

Lot of good her self-control and his qualifications did her now that her house was a charred ruin. When her father found out, he'd reel her in like one of his trophy game fish, bragging how right he'd been about a woman's inability to stand on her own. Never mind it wasn't her fault her one chance to prove her father wrong had gone up in smoke.

The truck hit a pothole and Tess bounced against her seatbelt. If Roman St. John knew the extent of the damage he'd done her, he'd probably get an *I told you so* in there as well, even though the fire was his crew's fault.

The truck bounded over another of the defects bad weather and poor maintenance had gouged into the country road. She grabbed the dash to steady herself. St. John's eyes glittered in the low light off the instrument panel and he pressed his foot to the accelerator.

"Having second thoughts?" he asked. "I'll gladly turn around and drive you back to town."

"You wish," she fired back at him, automatically contradicting anything this latest man seemingly hell-bent on dictating to her suggested, even if what he suggested was more reasonable…and safer.

"You being used to five star accommodations, I wouldn't want you to be disappointed." The near corner of his mouth twitched.

No doubt about it. Roman St. John enjoyed tormenting her. But he was in for a surprise if he thought a little mocking would send her running, tail-tucked between her legs. *Take over* and *take care of the little woman* type men had mocked her all her life.

Granted, none with as manly a physique as Roman St. John. Definitely not one she had to fight to resist. Damn the man his amazing looks, smug comebacks, and ability to aggravate her with seemingly little effort. Though she had to admit, she'd often found sparring with Roman an entertaining exercise. The one perk to having taken on a defensive demeanor with him.

"Just keep driving, St. John."

He wheeled the truck hard off the county road onto a dirt driveway and hit the brakes. Tess lurched against her seatbelt.

"Is it necessary to take every turn as though we're trying to out-maneuver someone tailing us?" she asked.

"My driving not five star enough for you, Princess?"

She scowled at the man slanting a self-satisfied smile her way. "I've told you before and I'll tell you again. No one calls me princess."

"I'd have bet everyone did."

"That's a bet you'd have lost, St. John."

He shifted in his seat and draped an arm along the back of the seat, an arm that was bare below the rolled back cuff of a plaid cotton shirt. Damned if she couldn't feel the heat emanating from that almost naked limb sprawled across the seatback and the small space between them.

Safer to go to a motel.

Involuntarily, her head tilted toward that heat, her hair brushing his skin. In spite of his offending her, she wanted to know the cradle of that arm. She wanted to be possessed by its strength—wanted to be possessed by the strength of the whole man. And therein lay the real danger of Roman St. John. She shouldn't want to be possessed by any man.

Definitely safer…a motel.

"Here we are," he all but sang in his smooth baritone, sweeping a broad hand toward the small structure caught in the arc of the truck's headlights. "Home sweet home."

That patronizing smugness that reminded her too much of her father, that was the real reason she refused what her body craved. That's why she'd declared Roman St. John off limits the day she realized he'd have made The Castle his family home. Not that he was wrong to have seen a *home* in the mansion. She'd seen it, too. But her target client wanted old elegance with all the modern conveniences. That was the client with the money to pay for the showcase she'd created. Yet, a tiny part of her was saddened to have taken away some of the original intent from so grand a house.

She shook off the thought because it was a sentiment she and Roman shared. Not that she'd ever admit such a thing to the man. She didn't even want to acknowledge it to herself. Such commonality only added another dimension to the chemical attraction she already had for a man. The last thing she needed was more reason to be drawn to a man who thought like her father. She was, above all, a woman who intended never to marry.

#

She was scowling. She was looking at his house and scowling. Roman should be glad. Surely now she'd admit she'd rather stay in a motel. But he resented her attitude. He'd built this house from the ground up. He was proud of it.

"Finding it a little small for your five star tastes?" he asked.

"It's smaller than my father's garage."

"It's no castle," he growled, instantly regretting reminding her of the house that he was likely responsible for making uninhabitable, "But it's livable enough for us *common* folk."

Her eyes narrowed at him. "You think I'm a spoiled rich girl, don't you?"

"If the glass slipper fits."

"Don't know your fairytales very well, either, do you?" she stated more than asked.

A man didn't grow up in a family of five kids and dote on a preschooler nephew without learning his fairytales. The fact was the woman pushed his buttons, made him forget to use reason. Made him act like a Neanderthal. It was that ever-contradicting mouth of hers...and that lean, firm body. Even shaking a finger at him as she did now, nothing on her body jiggled.

"Cinderella wasn't rich," she said. "She wasn't indulged and she wasn't a princess."

"Then make it a Gucci pump," he barked. "Just let me drive you to the best motel in town."

She huffed. "I have only the clothes on my back and no way to pay for anything."

"I'll pay for the room. I'll buy you a change of clothes."

"Not good enough."

"Why?"

"Because it's *your* crew's fault my house went up in flames tonight."

"Your house didn't *go up in flames*. Only the third floor burned."

"Because of the carelessness of one of *your* workers."

She had him there, if the Fire Marshal's investigation confirmed what the Fire Chief suspected.

"Look," he ventured, "we're both stressed out. Maybe there's a condo available at the ski hill. It's off season."

"I'm staying in your house."

"Why?"

She folded her arms across her chest, as stubborn a pose as she'd ever presented him. "Because you said if you didn't have my remodeling job done by the end of the week, I could move into your house. It's the end of the week, St. John, and my remodeling job isn't done. Not by a long shot. Now, are you a man of your word or not?"

Above all else, he was a man of his word.

"Fine." he said, slumping into his seat. "I'll leave the headlights on until you get on the porch."

She peered through the windshield and frowned. "You don't even have a paved walkway up to the house?"

"Dirt path's good enough for us peasants," he muttered.

She craned her neck as though searching the shadows beyond the reach of the headlights. "It is awfully dark out here."

Did he detect a hint of anxiety in her voice, an edge of uncertainty? Could Her-City-Born-Highness be uncomfortable with the dark? His shoulders lifted with the hope she might yet give in to reason and let him take her back to town. Maybe a few chosen facts of rural living would help persuade her out of staying under his roof tonight.

"Yep," he said in response to her comment about the darkness. "No pesky streetlights shining in our eyes and keeping us awake out here in God's country."

She scowled at him. But, as her gaze slid past him toward the woods edging the yard, apprehension pulled at her features. He should be kind. Ease up on her. But a knockout gorgeous harpy was the last thing he needed sleeping under his roof.

"With the extra overcast tonight," he said, "it'll be especially nice and dark."

She shivered and Roman felt a twinge of guilt. But he reminded himself who he was feeling guilty over and prodded, "Let me help you with your seatbelt."

Her hand clamped down on the belt buckle, her white knuckled fingers confirming that Little-Miss-Thinks-the-World-is-at-Her-Beck-and-Call wasn't as self-assured as she pretended. Again, guilt niggled at him.

"I can manage on my own, thank you," she retorted in the terse tone she'd used on him far too often in the past weeks as she released the seatbelt.

Suspecting she was bluffing, he offered, "Perhaps her Ladyship would like me to escort her to the door."

"That won't be necessary. I can manage—"

"On your own?"

"Yes," she snapped, opening the passenger side door.

"Of course," he returned, silently damning her stubborn-to-the-core tenacity. Why else would a woman *accustomed to five star accommodations* hold him to a stupid boast made in the heat of an argument?

She swung her legs out the door and slid to the ground, so petite she all but disappeared beyond the edge of the seat. He wished *she'd* disappear.

She peered across the bench seat at him, her eyes narrowed. "I have your word you'll leave the lights on until I'm up to the house?"

"Cross my heart and hope to die," he said.

"Hope to die, huh?" A tiny smile twitched at the corners of her lips. "Is that a promise?"

Damn, but the woman had a quick wit.

"If you still doubt my word at this point," he said, "let me put it another way. I wouldn't want her Ladyship to trip on a rut and have another reason to sue me."

She arched a shapely, dark eyebrow at him. "Sue you?"

Roman winced. The last thing he'd meant to do was remind her about what course of action she could take against him over the fire. As if he bought for a moment she hadn't already thought of it. She probably had her lawyer's phone number on speed dial.

"Just keep in mind," he said, "I offered to walk you to the door."

"What a gentleman."

Before he could retort that he *was* a gentleman, that she'd *know* it if she wasn't so quick with her razor-edged tongue, she shut the truck door. So much for scaring the mule-headed woman off with rough roads, dark woods, and bungalow-sized accommodations.

Maybe she wanted to make him squirm. That would be right up her alley or, in *her* case, boulevard. Maybe she'd give in and let him drive her back to town...once she crossed his threshold and invaded his territory.

Fine. Let the princess have her way. The sooner she saw how spare his accommodations were, the sooner he got rid of her...even if a part of him was going to miss their sparring matches. Strange, how their disagreements often felt as much like foreplay as arguments.

He watched her walk toward the house, the sway of her gently rounded hips all too well defined by her form-fitting running shorts.

"Ah, hell," he muttered. How could plain old physical attraction tie him up in such knots?

The second Tess' foot came down on the top step he flicked off the headlights and headed for the house, following the path he knew by heart. A twig snapped beneath his foot at the base of the steps.

"Is that you, St. John?" she asked from the porch.

"No, it's the bogey man," he said, focused on separating his house key from the rest on his key chain as he climbed the steps to the porch in the dark and...ran smack dab into his unwanted houseguest.

She screeched and tottered. He caught her by the

upper arm, his knuckles brushing the side of one firm, spandex-cupped breast. She swatted at him.

He let go of her as if she were a hot potato. "Did it ever occur to you to move out of the way?"

Her fingers snagged his sleeve and she groused and stumbled along at his side as he crossed the porch to the front door. "You turned off the lights too soon. I didn't have a chance to get my bearings."

"You're on my porch. It has a railing." He slid the key into the lock and turned it. "You couldn't have fallen off or gotten lost if you'd tried."

Her fingers bit into his sleeve, tugging the fabric over his arm. She really was unnerved. Another twinge of guilt nagged at him. He *should* reassure her. Maybe slip an arm around her and pull her close— protect her against whatever frightened her. But he needed to keep things professional. She'd clearly drawn that line between them the day they'd met face-to-face. If only she'd keep her mouth shut.

"There's a ramp off the end there," she said, a whisper of movement suggesting she gestured toward the side of his porch. "I could have been dumped right back into the driveway."

"Then you could sue me over that, too," he growled as he opened the door, reached inside, and flicked on an interior light.

"I didn't say I was going to sue you over anything—"

He eyed her hopefully, the light wedging out from the open door softening her features, making her appear anything but the she-devil he knew her to be. And she *was* a she-devil even if the diffused light made her eyes glint more with amusement than vindictiveness as she finished her statement about suing him with a smug, "—yet."

#

Chin held high and shoulders squared, Tess released Roman's shirtsleeve and stepped into his house. The entrance opened into a space between a kitchen with glistening, clutter free countertops and a front room with nary a magazine out of place. Apparently, St. John didn't spend much time here. No man was this neat. *Hell*, she wasn't this neat.

He crowded in behind her, a wall of rock hard muscle bumping against her shoulder blades. Odd, how they tended to bump into each other more than two coordinated people ought. Aunt Honey would have called those encounters Freudian slips of the physical kind—Aunt Honey who had listened to her complaints about Roman's tendency to get in her way...and about how he wore his tool belt slung way too low on his hips.

Never mind that the belt was designed for a carpenter's convenience. The way the hammer handle thumped against the man's thigh with his every move, the smooth stroke of his hand in and out of the nail pocket center front, and the ready release of the clip-on tape measure got her thinking on something far removed from construction. Even now, just the thought of that belt and its dangling hammer handle...

"Unless you want to spend the night entertaining mosquitoes," he said, close enough that his breath whispered against the back of her ear, "I'd suggest you move out of the way and let me close the door."

So much for fantasies. Besides, she didn't need him or any other man to fulfill her dreams. She would build her own empire one refurbished house at a time...provided men like Roman St. John quit burning up her assets.

"How inconvenient of me to be in your way, St.

John," she mewed, stepping into the front room—
rubbing the tickle of his breath from her ear and
adding over her shoulder, "but then, I wouldn't be
here at all if my house hadn't been set ablaze by one
of your employees."

He grumbled something under his breath she no
doubt didn't want to hear. As if the opinion of any
man who owned a plaid couch could be of importance
to her.

A photo on a table beside the couch of a woman
with wildly curling strawberry-blond locks and a little
boy with straight wheat-hued hair caught her eye.
Tess picked up the picture and studied it closer,
frowning as she compared the color of the child's hair
to Roman's. He'd never said anything about being a
father...or being married...or having been married.

Not that she'd ever asked. She hadn't. Nor did she
have a reason to. And she never would. It didn't
concern her. A woman who had no intentions of
marrying didn't need to know such things about a
man.

But a man who never spoke of his child was not a
man she could respect.

"That's my sister and her son, Ben," he said.

So much for assumptions. A smile pulled at her
lips and she set the picture down. Not that she had
any business being pleased that her contractor wasn't
married. It was just her bad luck her heart lurched
into her throat every time she looked into his
Icelandic blue eyes.

Even if he *was* a spectacular specimen of
manhood, he was too much like her father. At least he
was whenever he espoused the merits of family life.

Then again, maybe all she saw in those eyes was
a man she dared not allow too close. Much as she

hated to admit her father was right about anything, he'd pegged her when he said she always wanted what she couldn't have.

"Now what are you scowling at?" Roman demanded.

Tess blinked, and when the heavy dark lashes lifted once more, his uninvited houseguest's gaze fixed on his hand clamped over the edge of the still open door. "I thought the object of my getting out of your way was so you could close the door and keep out the mosquitoes."

He stepped into the room toward her, silently cursing her pig-headedness as he slammed the door shut behind him. The object had been to crowd her—push her to realize she'd manipulated herself into being alone in the home of a man she barely knew…and to make her see the error of her actions. Instead, the inimitable Tess Abbott had pushed him into closing them in his house alone together.

Worse, she strolled deeper into his house, her hips swaying. His palms could almost feel their perfect fit. On the brink of the hall that housed the stairway to the second level and split the rear of the house, her crisp voice trailed back at him.

"You going to give me the grand tour, or shall I explore on my own?"

He should have known Tess was beyond reasoning with. She'd proven that all too often in the past weeks while working on her house—a house he knew far better than she did. Yet, his every suggestion was met with argument.

Maybe that was the key to handling her, reverse psychology.

But, when he focused once more on her, she stood at the base of the steps just outside his bedroom. Tess Abbot in Spandex shorts and form-fitting tank top mere feet from the foot of his bed. Reverse psychology called for him to suggest she take his room—sleep in his bed. Hell, she and her trim runner's body were already *too close* to his bed for *his* peace of mind.

That wouldn't work. Not for him. Certainly not with her. She was flat out too clever to fall for reverse psychology. Her quick wit was proof enough of that. And she was smart. He liked that she'd known how to open up a supporting wall without dropping the roof into the front room—liked that he could use builder's lingo and she understood what he was talking about.

He liked way too much about Tess Abbot to let her into his bed…whether or not he shared it with her.

"That's *my* bedroom," he said, sounding more territorial than he'd intended.

"Is this the *one and only* bedroom in the house?"

"And if it is?"

She folded her arms across her chest and leaned against the doorframe, her eyes gleaming. "Then you better hope that plaid couch of yours is comfy, because that's where you'll be sleeping."

"You think you're entitled to the prime location, huh?"

"When I've been rooted out of my house due to no fault of my own, I expect the offending party to be gracious about living up to what he promised."

"I offered only that you could move into my house. I said nothing about moving into my bedroom."

He advanced on her until he towered over her. She didn't flinch. He'd give her points for hutzpah.

"St. John, you should know by now you can't intimidate me."

He should have known such tactics wouldn't work considering how often she'd backed him down already during the remodeling of The Castle.

She nodded over her shoulder at the stairs climbing from outside his bedroom door. "What's up there?"

"My office is upstairs...and a second bedroom."

"Second bedroom, huh?" She straightened between the doorframe and him, peered up into the darkness above, and flicked the light switch on.

"Does it have a bed?" she asked.

"Yes."

"Terrific. I'll take that room." She lifted her face at his, lifted it so close he could smell the minty sweetness of her breath through the clinging smokiness of the fire. "And you thought I couldn't be reasonable."

"Uncle," he said, taking a step back.

"Excuse me?"

"I'm crying *uncle*. Anything to get you to let me drive you back to town and put you up in a nice room anywhere else but here."

A smile slanted across her mouth, causing tiny dimples to dent the corners of her sinfully lush lips. "Just point me in the direction of your bathtub, St. John."

Bathtub? Swell. Not only was he about to be stuck under the same roof with Tess Abbot for the night, she was about to get *naked*.

CHAPTER TWO

He motioned her past the stairway toward a partially open door beyond the kitchen. When Tess paused in the doorway, he reached around her and flicked on the light, crowding her into the brightly tiled room in the process. "There're extra towels on the—"

She stepped into the room, turned and shut the door in his face. He'd been about to follow her into the bathroom. Imagine, her and Roman St. John, confined in this narrow space together—that towering man with the linebacker shoulders and feet half the size of the state of Illinois. He'd probably have knocked her into the tub.

Unless he caught her with those huge hands of his, like he had when he'd bumped into her on the porch. Such big, strong hands. She wondered if what they said about the size of a man's hands and feet being indicative of the size of another anatomical attribute was true.

"Don't go there. Don't go there. Just don't go there," she chanted in a low voice and thumped her head back against the bathroom door.

"You okay in there?"

She spun at the door. The man was still out there, right *outside* the door. She flicked the lock into place. "I'm just fine. I don't need a chaperone to bathe."

"I heard a thump. I was concerned. So, shoot

me."

Wasn't that a thought? As if resolving this whole mess could be accomplished so simply. But there were laws against shooting a person just because he bothered you.

She could hear him mumbling on the other side of the door. Then his footsteps faded off down the hall, heavy, hurried steps.

Tess rolled her head, the tension crackling in her ears like popcorn. She needed a good long soak in a tub of hot water and not just because her clothes and hair smelled of smoke.

She drew back the shower curtain, not surprised to find a sparkling tub. He had to have cleaning help…or a woman in his life. She frowned at that last thought. She frowned deeper at wasting even a second trying to recall if he'd ever mentioned a woman during his weeks working in her house. Not that Roman's eligibility status was of any concern to a woman who'd sworn off matrimony, even if the man in question had a disarmingly good-natured streak. She'd witnessed almost as much bantering between him and his crew as she did good quality work.

She plugged the drain, turned on the hot water, and scanned the back lip of the tub for bath supplies. She wanted bubbles. Not that she expected to find bubble bath among her reluctant host's paraphernalia. A man like Ro—

Whoa. What was this?

Between a nondescript lump of soap and a *Value Size* jug of shampoo stood a bottle whose label identified it as bubbling bath crystals. Before she could censure herself, an image of her contractor popped into her head, his brawny arms draped along the sides of the tub while one hairy leg protruded from a pile of iridescent suds. Maybe the man *was* right about her coming home with him being a bad idea. She was attracted to him. She lusted after him. Of course it was a bad idea.

But she refused to admit it to him. That would be like admitting defeat to her father.

Tess scowled, dumped a hefty amount of bath crystals under the stream of water spilling from the spout, and turned toward the open shelves above the toilet stacked with towels. They were a motley collection of odd sizes and dark colors, mostly burgundy. She wouldn't have pegged him for a man with enough imagination to waver from the standard blues she expected of men who wore plaid shirts. Then again, he had surprised her a few times in the past weeks.

Curious if she'd find other surprises in the personal space of his bathroom, she opened a set of bi-fold doors opposite the tub and sink and found a washer and dryer. Compact and orderly with a shelf of laundry supplies above the appliances. Even the dirty clothes hadn't been tossed willy-nilly. They were in a laundry basket atop the washing machine, Roman St. John's white, rumpled shorts and sweaty, navy tees.

What was she doing fingering his t-shirts? She should be repulsed. They bore the sweat of a man who labored hard. And he did. She'd seen him, swinging his hammer and hefting massive beams, making the muscles bunch across his back beneath the tight weave of his t-shirt.

She shook off the image and concentrated on the reality at hand…like smelly shirts. But his tees didn't reek of stale sweat. They smelled of the male essence of the last man on earth to whom she dared be attracted.

"What are you doing?" she muttered, holding one of his t-shirts to her nose and inhaling.

Torturing myself, that's what I'm doing.

She tossed the shirt back into the basket and paced the narrow bathroom. Steam wafted from her filling bath, inviting her into the water. Yet, she couldn't resist snooping further.

The cabinet under the sink held the usual cleaning supplies. The medicine cabinet above housed a spare supply of bandages, aspirin, floss—which accounted for Roman St. John's brilliant white teeth—and shaving cream and razor.

She picked up the razor and turned it between her fingers. Her father used the electric version. No raw stainless steel blades threatening his pampered cheeks, unless the blade was wielded by a barber whose business it was to know the definitive cutting angle of a straight razor.

She had the distinct impression that her contractor had never wasted a minute of his time worrying about a little razor burn. At least he and her father differed in that way.

But in other ways…

Once he questioned the wisdom of knocking out a wall between two bedrooms to make a grand master suite. Like she didn't know downgrading from five to four bedrooms meant value lost. She'd promptly pointed out she was no rooky architect. That she knew what she was doing—knew her target market and they wanted big masters. He'd complied with her design plan in the end. Not that he had a choice, as she'd also pointed out *she* was the client.

She slapped the razor back on the shelf and all but slammed the medicine cabinet door. She knew what she was doing and why, even if her contractor didn't approve of her design. But she didn't have the luxury of time to wait for a buyer who'd appreciate the integrity of small, Victorian era rooms. She needed that house remodeled to the esthetic preferred by the upscale buyer, and she needed it on the market ASAP.

A whiff of smoke wafted up off her clothes. With The Castle a charred, water-logged ruin, there would be no sale, speedy or otherwise. So much for proving to her father that a woman was as capable in this business as a man, thanks to Roman and his band of merry men.

"Forget St. John," she muttered, stripping off her clothes. "Forget him and his amazing blue eyes, muscled arms, and…and his damn burgundy towels."

She sank into the hot bath, trying not to think about his very broad shoulders in bubbles. She needed to unwind so she could think this latest problem through without letting her emotions muddle the process. Any decision emotion based could only prove her father right about women not belonging in business.

#

Roman stared at the wall above the stove as he sliced an onion into a hot skillet, the wall that partitioned the kitchen from the bathroom. The water had stopped running and he swore he could actually hear her *sinking* into the bathwater. But that was impossible. He'd insulated these walls himself. Had to be his imagination and under-used of late libido picturing Tess Abbot in the buff climbing into his bathtub.

The knife slipped and sliced into the pad of his thumb.

"Damn!"

He scowled at the blood bubbling along the thin cut. First aid kit was in the bathroom…where the inhospitable Miss Abbot soaked naked in his tub. He wondered if she'd used his bath salts, if she was buried up to her stubborn little chin in suds.

He cursed again and tossed the knife and onion remnant onto the countertop next to the stove. If his thumb were hanging by a cord and blood spurting from an artery, he wouldn't knock on that bathroom door for her help. Nope. No way. No how.

"Get that notion out of your head right now, Roman my man, because the acid-tongued Tess is strictly off limits."

He wrapped a paper napkin around his thumb then retrieved a platter of meat from the fridge. All day he'd anticipated eating the sirloin steak he'd seasoned last night and left marinating. He'd planned to celebrate the end of working with the impossible Ms. Abbott with that hunk of meat. That is until her third floor caught on fire, flames devouring her roof and the billowing smoke making her house look like a smudge pot.

That quickly, a job done had turned into a new nightmare. Instead of putting the client from hell behind him, he now had her as a houseguest. To add insult to injury, he had to cut his steak in half and share it with his uninvited houseguest.

A loud splash drew his attention back to the wall behind the stove and spurred his imagination into a space it had no business visiting, not when that space involved soapy bubbles and a fresh-faced harpy. Had she slipped? He banged the platter down next to the knife and cursed yet again, a speech pattern he seemed to be using with far more frequency since starting work for the tyrannical Tess.

She could drown in there for all he cared, considering what she'd put him through. Still, he listened for movement, just in case. Given their none-too-private verbal sparring, an accident might not be the first cause of death the local sheriff suspected. And her family? They'd want to know what she was doing naked in his tub first then they would sue him for so much he'd owe them his soul.

But, if he scooped Tess Abbot's unconscious body—slick with soap—from the tub and breathed life into it, he'd be a hero. Tess might even say something nice to him.

Running water trickled beyond the wall between bath and kitchen and his fantasy evaporated.

"You are pathetic," he muttered into the stinging vapor of frying onions and potatoes.

His stomach rumbled in protest. He hadn't eaten all day. He'd been too busy scrambling to finish the last minute changes her royal pain in the butt had wanted. For a woman who found his company so irritating she couldn't say a nice word to him to save her soul, she sure found ways to keep him on the job longer.

His stomach growled again and he eyed the steak. What if she was a vegetarian?

If she were, he might as well go ahead and cook the steak for himself. No sense his starving while she took her sweet time soaking her pampered backside.

An image of Tess Abbot's skin flushed from steamy bathwater popped into his head. Immediately, he shook his head, shaking away the image. He had no business knocking on that bathroom door just to find out her food preference. Besides, it would be nice to eat *with* someone for change.

Was he nuts? He was talking about the vixen with a tongue like a switchblade. Better he eat alone.

#

The knock on the door jolted Tess from her peace.

"What?" she demanded.

"How long are you going to be in there?"

Wasn't there a man on earth capable of giving a woman five minutes of peace?

"You got a hot date to get ready for, St. John?"

"I want to know when to put the steak on."

"Steak? Swell. My house burns down and you barbecue. What is it with you men and your barbecues?"

"If you don't eat meat—"

"My father barbecues a few hamburgers and hot dogs," she ranted, "and he expects the world to stand up and applaud."

"If you're not a meat eater," he growled through a door with too flimsy a lock to keep out a strapping contractor if he wanted in, "I should tell you I don't have an ounce of tofu in the house."

"Like you'd know what to do with bean curd if you had any."

"Care to bet on that?"

Tess frowned and muttered above the grumble of her stomach, "Something tells me that would be a sucker bet."

Why was she wasting time arguing with this guy when a steak sounded so good to her? A big, thick, rare steak.

"When you hear the water draining from the tub, St. John," she shouted at the door, "you can slap the meat on the grill."

"Helpful," he muttered. "Real helpful."

Tess heard his footsteps as he departed and sank back into the suds with a groan. Why were men so quick to take offense to a woman who knew her own mind? Why did men think they had to run her life?

Why couldn't her father see she was as capable an architect as any of the men in his firm? But no, Dad refused to see women in any career but that of a homemaker and mother.

"A woman's duty is in the home," he'd said so many times she couldn't believe she'd not recognized the futility of fighting his closed mind earlier.

She should have at least caught on when she'd graduated from college with honors and he'd said, "Wasn't there one man in the whole architectural department you could have married?"

She'd thought he merely needed educating. So she'd begged her way into his firm and accepted every menial task he'd assigned her, or rather he'd had other architects in the firm assign her. She'd bitten the bullet, telling herself he didn't want to show favoritism, that he was testing her—making her stronger. She thought she would be the woman to prove to her father that women could do it all.

By the time Harry Dawson joined the firm, she'd started to notice that drafts*men* with less experience and lesser schooling were getting promoted ahead of her. Over Manhattan Iced Teas, she and Harry had commiserated over her father's lack of support of her and Harry's less than stellar design skills. The next thing she knew, they were in bed together and Dad was inviting Harry to Sunday dinners.

She finally had her father's attention. The day Harry produced a diamond engagement ring he couldn't possibly afford on his salary, it had taken very little investigation on her part to uncover why

Harry had gotten a substantial raise, and why he was being lauded as the firm's newest rising star. The design Harry had presented to her father, the design that landed the firm a large government contract had been *hers. He'd stolen her work.*

But Harry's betrayal was minimal next to her father's. When she'd presented him with the evidence of Harry's double-dealing, the least she'd expected her father to do was fire Harry. Instead, dear old dad chastised her for undermining her future husband, pointing out Harry had people skills. He had connections. So, what was the big deal if she helped her husband-to-be with his designs now and then?

What was the big deal?

The big deal was that daddy-dearest saw her only as a means to bring a *son*-in-law into the family business when he should have been grooming his daughter to take over. That's when she ended her engagement to Harry and resigned from the firm, refusing to comply with her father's twenty-first century version of an arranged marriage.

Just her luck the man she'd hired to renovate her first project seemed to have the same outdated inclinations about family and marriage as her father. A man with forever etched all over his baby blues. A man with an outdated bias was no man for her. Besides, she wasn't looking for forever with any man.

The gall of Roman St. John pounding on her door when she was trying to unwind from the catastrophe for which he was to blame. And for what reason? To demand she give him a time when she'd be done so he could cook his steak.

"Inconsiderate, self-serving—" Opening the drain, she climbed out of the tub. There'd be no more relaxing, thanks to Roman St, John. Never mind that her stomach growled with the ferocity of a lioness five days from her last meal.

She grabbed up her clothes and the smell of smoke slapped her in the face. She threw the garments back on the floor and scanned the small room for something else to wear. There was nothing...unless she wanted to don one of St. John's sweaty t-shirts.

"Men! They expect us to be at their beck and call, to look our best and smile pretty. To make sure their shirts are pressed and their three-minute eggs are cooked to perfection! But can even one of them have the forethought to set out a robe for a woman?"

#

She entered the kitchen in a puff of steam and a pair of towels, one wrapped around her head and the other around her torso, barely covering the most intimate parts of Tess's personal terrain.

"The least you could have done was put a robe in the bathroom for me," she said none-too politely.

Roman blinked at the enticing swell of breasts visible above the edge of a maroon towel and blankly repeated, "Robe?"

"You can't expect me to put my smoky clothes back on?"

Dumbly, he shook his head. It wasn't like he'd never seen a woman in a towel before. He was a man of some experience, the sort of experience he'd recently put on hold as a courtesy to the future Mrs. St. John, whomever she might be. But, he'd never seen Tess Abbot in a towel.

Or experienced such mixed feelings at the same time. On one level, he was being chewed out and resented it. On another, he wanted her, harpy mouth and all.

He tore his gaze away from her breasts and looked at her mouth in an attempt to break the spell. Bad choice. He wanted to press his lips to hers, if only to shut her up.

Wrong. He wanted to possess those lush lips, and plunder her mouth with his tongue. To tear the towel from her body, swipe the dishes off the table, and take her right there amidst scattered utensils and spilled salad.

"A robe, St. John?" she prompted, hands on hips.

How could such terse words make those full, bow-shaped lips look so inviting? It had to be abstinence that had him lusting after the bane of his existence, and the sweetly compact breasts and forever legs within reach. He shouldn't have looked down. The woman had legs that climbed from ten red-painted toenails to eternity. And eternity was where he wanted to be right now.

He groaned and headed for his bedroom, his voice oddly hoarse in his ears. "I'll find you something to wear."

Roman breezed past her, ordering, "Keep an eye on the steak."

"You expect me to go outside dressed like this?" Tess turned after him, flipping an edge of the towel wrapped around her torso.

He paused in the doorway of his bedroom and looked back at her, a perplexed expression on his face...until his eyes followed the flick of the towel against her thigh. Something more carnal flickered across the baby blues then. Oh yeah, her contractor was definitely the typical lusting male. Men were so predictable.

"Steak's under the broiler," he said through clenched teeth before disappearing into the bedroom.

She gave him credit for not leering as she moved to the stove and peeked inside the oven. Two slabs of beef sizzled under the broiler. So, he didn't exactly *barbecue*. Another plus?

She plucked a morsel from the frying pan on top of the stove and popped it into her mouth. As she rolled the hot potato around her tongue to cool it, she studied the table set with two place settings. Forks on the left, knives and spoons on the right. So, he wasn't a total barbarian, either.

She chewed, her mouth flooding with flavors. She plucked another tidbit from the pan, blew on it this time before sampling. There was more than just salt and pepper and potato teasing her taste buds. So, the man could cook, too.

Wanting more, she scooped another piece from the frying pan, scorching her fingers this time and dropping the potato slice. Reflexively, she stuck her burnt fingers into her mouth just as he emerged from his bedroom.

She was sucking on her fingers. Tess Abbot, razor-tongued temptress, was standing in his kitchen in a skimpy towel sucking on her fingers. Whatever had he done in life to deserve this kind of punishment?

Roman fixed his gaze on her eyes, determined not to notice how her full lips looked suctioned around two of her fingers—how they rounded in an almost surprised "oh" shape that didn't quite match the devilment in her eyes. He stopped just out of reach of the woman...a man could be tempted only so far...and dangled a t-shirt and sweat-shorts with a drawstring waistband in front of her.

"I don't have a robe," he said.

One corner of those finger-sucking lips lifted.

"Try these," he offered, hoping she didn't hear the pleading behind his words. Being how immune to him she seemed to be, he wasn't keen on her seeing how weak his libido was.

She removed her fingers from her mouth, cocked her head to one side, and smiled a crooked, little smile. Oh, she knew exactly what effect she had him. He drew a bolstering breath and waited for the inevitable smart-alecky come-back. But she said nothing. She just tugged the shorts and shirt from his fingers and sauntered off down the hall, her hips swaying beneath the thin terrycloth towel. Damn but that woman had moves that could cause a ten-car pile-up.

She glanced back at him just then, one hand on the bathroom doorframe, and said, "You cook a mean potato, St. John."

"Am I to take that as a compliment?"

"Take it however you like," she said through puckered lips. Then she was gone, the bathroom door closed between them.

Take it however he liked, huh? Well, what he liked might not be quite what she had in mind. But then, he wasn't thinking about the potatoes. He was thinking about that towel slipping off her high, rounded breasts and sliding down her forever long legs to pool on the floor around her perfectly painted toenails. He was thinking about her stepping into his shorts, and about his t-shirt sliding down over her head, her shoulders, and her—

He smelled smoke.

Tess had bathed. She clearly wasn't wearing her smoky clothes. The scent of smoke couldn't possibly have come from her. Maybe it was him.

But, before he could sniff his shirtsleeve, a curl

of smoke drifted past his nose from the direction of the stove. With a curse, he pulled the steak charring beneath a blistering broiler from the oven. What more could go wrong for him today?

#

Tess closed the upstairs bedroom door behind her, leaned back against it, and smoothed Roman's t-shirt down over her full stomach. They'd eaten without talking until she couldn't bear the silence. So, she'd complimented him again on his potatoes.

"It's the sweet onions and minced garlic that give them a bite," he'd replied.

Sweet onions? Minced garlic? She was only vaguely aware of there being a variety of onions as she'd rarely joined her mother and sisters in the kitchen. The man not only knew about onions, but he *minced* garlic as well. A domesticated man. Her father would not approve of that.

But did she?

She tugged the neck of Roman's t-shirt up to her nose and inhaled the tangy aroma of seared beef. He'd taken the worst burnt piece of sirloin and given her the choicest piece. Trying to impress her? Or was he just being a good host?

The t-shirt he'd given her to wear wasn't one of the thin, blue undershirts he normally wore under his plaid shirts, either. Instead he'd given her a sturdier, navy blue version with a whimsical figure of a carpenter stamped on the front. She'd have called such an act chivalrous, were she a romantic woman.

But she wasn't.

Tess slid the ribbed neckband of the t-shirt across her lips and contemplated the man to whom the shirt belonged, a man who did not own a robe. Why did that make her smile?

Because men in robes tended to look stuffy and Roman St. John was anything but stuffy. Besides, he had far too wonderful a chest as defined by those thin blue tees to hide beneath a robe.

Or a pajama top.

As if what he wore or didn't wear to bed should matter to her. He was not for her, plain and simple.

Then why was she relishing the differences between him and her father? Why couldn't she stop searching for his scent among the navy blue threads of the t-shirt? Why was she contemplating how best to find out what Roman St. John wore to bed...if he wore anything at all?

Her gaze fixed on the double bed tucked under the peak of the roof. Stomach full, bubble bath fresh, and feeling quite toasty in Roman's over-sized t-shirt, it was only natural that her mind wander to the one area where she remained yet unsated.

And to be sated, all she had to do was descend the steps to the bedroom directly beneath hers. Yep. Bat the eyelashes a few times and give him a come-hither look or two, and her reluctant host would be at her mercy.

Yeah, right. His eyes all but bugged out of head and his tongue nearly rolled across the floor   like some lusting cartoon wolf when he'd seen her in that towel. But she doubted Roman would welcome any invitation from her. She'd tweaked his ego far too often. Never mind she'd done it to keep him at bay. A woman who intended never to marry hadn't any business tempting a man looking for a wife. Business being the operative word here. And business was the only thing that should be on her mind.

How she was going to repair The Castle in time to sell it before that balloon payment at the end of the year. Six months wasn't a lot of time, especially when she had no idea how much damage had been done to The Castle, let alone how long it would take to repair it.

Yawning, she shucked the bulky shorts and kicked them aside. The bottom of the t-shirt tumbled halfway down her thighs, its caress reminding her of Roman's broad hands with their callused fingers—fingers whose firm yet non-bruising grip had earlier on the porch kept her upright. How nice it would be to enlist his help with the repairs.

Wrong.

Even if St. John wasn't exactly like her father, he was the second to last man on earth to whom she should turn for help, her father being the first.

She yawned again and eyed the double bed with its fluffy comforter. Clearly she was overly tired if she was contemplating asking Roman's help fixing The Castle. First thing in the morning, she'd inspect the house and determine the extent of damage.

She flicked off the switch beside the door for the overhead light and the room plunged into blackness. Immediately, Tess' body reacted. Her heart skipped a beat then began a familiar jack hammer dance. Her throat tightened. Sweat popped out along her spine. She switched the light back on.

Roman had warned her the nights were dark out here in the country. Maybe if she opened the drapes.

But the room's dormered window wasn't covered with draperies, curtains, or even a shade. She scowled, torn between the lack of privacy that bare window presented and its isolating blackness. She needed a nightlight.

But there was no reading lamp on the nightstand beside the bed or on the dresser beneath the window, just that harsh, glaring overhead fixture. How was she supposed to sleep with a hundred watts of light shining in her face?

#

Roman was aware of Tess the moment she stepped into his open doorway. He should have closed his bedroom door. He would from now on for as long as she insisted on inhabiting his spare bedroom.

But, at the moment, she stood in his doorway in his t-shirt but clearly no longer wearing his shorts. Did she know what she did to him, standing on the threshold of his bedroom with all that bare leg showing?

He lowered the book he was reading and demanded, "What?"

"There's no reading lamp in my room," she said.

"Can't you read by the overhead light?" he asked.

"I wasn't planning on reading."

"Then why do you need a reading lamp?"

She blinked, frowned briefly then peeked up at him through a heavy fringe of lashes. "In case I have to get up during the night." One corner of her mouth twitched. "You wouldn't want me tripping over anything, now would you? You wouldn't want me to have any additional reasons to sue you?"

Was she goading him, or flirting with him? Whichever, he refused to rise to the bait.

"Then leave the hall light on and your door open," he said.

She swept her little, round chin into its ever familiar imperial angle and pursed her lips. "I don't want to leave my door open."

He half expected her to stomp her foot...her little, perfect, bare foot with its painted nails. She should have stuck with the seductive approach. He might have succumbed to that. But the harpy tempted him to show her he could give as good as she gave.

"What's the matter, Princess," he said, bringing his gaze back up to her face, "you afraid an open door is more than my male libido can resist?"

She folded her arms over her chest, the cock of her chin more challenging now than imperial. "I should point out, St. John, I have a killer uppercut."

"Why doesn't that surprise me?"

"Because I'm a woman who can take care of myself, perhaps?"

"Or maybe because you're a lot like the woman in these pages." He wagged the book he held loosely in his lap. "She has a wallop that would stop any man in his tracks, too." *And a tongue to match.*

She looked at the book, no doubt curious to know who he was comparing her to. He palmed the book, hiding its faded title from her.

"I don't have a spare reading lamp," he said.

"How about a table lamp from the living room?"

"How about a flashlight?" he retorted.

Her shoulders drooped, a crease scored her broad brow, and her gaze dropped to the floor. She looked so uncertain he had the urge to gather her in his arms and promise everything would work out, and this wasn't the first time he'd had the urge to protect her. How did she do that, flip from harpy to vulnerable in a blink of the eye?

"Okay, St. John," she said, looking him in the eye. "Here's the facts. I need a nightlight. It's pitch black up there, and I've never slept without one."

The eyes blazing at him dared him to make something of her revelation. Little did she know he couldn't kick an opponent when she was down, harpy or not.

Roman tossed his book aside, threw back the covers, and slid out of bed. She glanced down the front of him and, for an instant, looked startled. Then a smile spread across those lips he'd have liked to sample, were she a sweeter sort of woman.

"What's the matter, Princess? Don't my pajama bottoms live up to your royal standards?"

"On the contrary. I think smiley faces are adorable." She grinned up at him as he stopped in front of her, her deep, brown eyes twinkling.

"They were a gift from my sister," he said. "A gag gift."

"And you wear them even though they were a gag?"

"Not wearing them would be a waste."

"Practical Roman," she said, tsking in a way that reminded him of his sister's own good-natured ribbing about his practicality. He wasn't sure he liked the shrewish Tess teasing him.

"I'll bring you a nightlight if you go wait for me in your bedroom."

She gave him a crooked smile, pivoted on her heel, and bounded up the steps.

All that leg wasted on a woman too ornery to live with. He shook his head, retrieved the nightlight from the kitchen junk drawer, and headed upstairs.

She was sitting on the bed, covers drawn up over the knees she hugged up under her chin. Thank goodness for that quilt. A man could take only so much tempting before he broke. Still, he couldn't help but speculate at what he'd find under that old quilted bedcover. How would Tess Abbot react if she knew what primal thoughts heated his blood?

Then he realized she was taking her own time

perusing his bare chest.

Run, urged a tiny voice inside his head. *Run fast and far.*

"Here." He thrust the nightlight at her, but she didn't take it. She just stared at it, eyebrows raised.

"A Winnie-the-Pooh nightlight?" Amusement laced her words.

"I bought it when my nephew visited."

"You babysat your nephew?"

"No, I eat little children. You'll find his bones in the bone pile out back. Jeez, Tess. What kind of man do you think I am? I'll plug in the nightlight for you." He dropped to one knee beside the dresser where there was an electrical outlet.

"Aren't you the gentleman," she all but purred from the bed.

"Anything your little heart desires, Princess," he grumbled, fighting the nightlight's bent prongs into the outlet.

"In that case, St. John—"

He rose and faced her, dread inching up his spine.

"—Turn off the overhead light on your way out…please."

That was it? No tirade about the Spartan accommodation, or the lack of curtains on the window? Even a *please?* He was almost disappointed.

"Sure," he said.

"And leave the hall light on…in case I get up during the night."

"Anything else Her Highness requires before her humble servant retires for the night?" he parried.

"I'll whistle if I think of anything."

"I just bet you will."

CHAPTER THREE

The third time Tess opened her eyes and squinted into the sunlight streaming through the bedroom's unclad window, she knew she wasn't having a nightmare. The lumpy bed beneath her and the slanted ceiling over her head were real, as real as yesterday's fire at The Castle.

Tess winced. She'd put everything she had into that project. She'd even had a couple prospective buyers interested, buyers expecting a livable house. Now what was she going to do?

She could call Aunt Honey and hash out options with her.

No, she couldn't. Not for the next three weeks. Aunt Honey had gone to a monastery somewhere in the Andes. Spiritual enlightenment was Aunt Honey's latest passion. No cell phones allowed. Besides, she needed to assess the damage at The Castle before she could determine any plan of action.

Tess climbed out of bed, slipped on Roman's shorts, and stumbled down the steps. Roman's door was shut. Obviously the fire for which he was responsible wasn't nagging Prince Charmless awake this morning. After all the times he'd hammered on her front door at the crack of dawn, it would serve him right if she returned the favor and knocked on his door right now.

She yawned. Maybe she'd do just that…right after she had her first cup of coffee.

She shuffled into the kitchen to the coffeemaker.

There was already coffee in it. Just enough to fill a mug. But the pot was cold. Yesterday's brew?

Not in Mr. Neat's domain.

Alarm tingled at the base of Tess' skull. If the cold coffee wasn't from yesterday—

She charged Roman's bedroom door and threw it open. No Roman. No happy face pjs. Just his made-up bed.

She dashed out the front door. The driveway was empty as well. He'd abandoned her. That countrified version of her father had up and stranded her in the woods!

Blood pounding in her ears, she stormed back into the house. A yellow sticky note on the kitchen table fluttered with her passing. She backed up and read it. It stated simply, "Taxi," followed by a phone number.

Okay. He hadn't stranded her.

She drew a deep breath in through her nose then blew it slowly out her mouth, a calming technique she'd learned in some long ago yoga class. She'd overreacted. Couple yesterday's emotional roller-coaster ride with not having had her eye-opening cup of coffee yet, it was no wonder. She'd feel better after she got her caffeine fix and some food.

She found a coffee mug, filled it from the cold pot, and stuck it in the microwave. The yellow sticky note with the cab number beckoned her from the table. It would take some time for a taxi to drive out here. She should call and set a time for them to pick her up.

She dialed the number. One ring. Two rings. The microwave timer went off. The long cord on the wall mounted phone let her reach the mug. Gratefully, she wrapped her fingers around the steamy cup.

Three rings.

She popped a couple slices of bread in the toaster.

Four rings.

The toaster lever jammed and she wiggled it.

Five rings.

What kind of cab company took this long to answer its phone? The toaster lever jerked loose and the bread popped up. She hammered the lever back down and the bread with it.

She was about to give up on the cab when a woman answered on the sixth ring, a baby squalling in the background. "I'm sorry," Tess said, "I must have called the wrong—"

The woman shouted over the caterwauling infant.

Tess pulled the receiver away from her ear, reiterating, "You *are* Penetti's Cab Company?" *Small towns and their casual business practices.* "I need a cab at—"

"I have to talk to your husband?" Tess asked with more than a little confusion. "Is he the dispatcher?"

Another shouted response, this time with the added backup of another child intoning, "Mommy. Mommy. Mommy."

"Your husband is the cabby. Okay." Tess rolled her eyes.

She sipped at her coffee as she waited for the husband to respond to the wife's shouts and come to the phone. These people would never make it in Chicago.

And what was that singed smell?

She zeroed in on the smoking toaster and tried to raise the burning bread, but the damned lever stuck again. She jerked the toaster cord from the outlet, accidentally hitting the toaster with her hand and sending it flying across the counter top. It crashed to the floor just as the cabby came on line.

"I need a cab," she said, flinging her coffee on the flaming toast now skidding across the inlaid. Just as the cabby spoke, the smoke detector in the hall squealed to life.

"Just a minute," she shouted into the mouthpiece, dragging a chair under the smoke detector. "Let me shut this thing up."

She tucked the phone receiver under her chin, climbed onto the chair, and dislodged the battery. But the alarm kept squealing at ear splitting decibels.

"It's hard wired," she muttered and cursed Roman's attention to code even though she would have been every bit as safety-conscious and connected the alarm directly to the house current.

She ripped the detector off the ceiling and the squeal gave way to an annoying blip. "Internal back up battery," she explained into the phone receiver. Roman had covered every base. "I'll just be another second."

She dropped from the chair, set the phone down, went to the front door, and flung the alarm outside. Silence once more reigning, she picked up the phone. "Now, about that cab."

"What do you mean the cab is in the shop? You can't possibly have just one—"

"You have only one cab and it's getting a new transmission today." She managed a tight, "Thank you," and hung up.

"You did this on purpose, Roman St. John. You left me the phone number of the lamest cab company in town."

She found a phone book in the nearest kitchen drawer and opened it to the yellow pages. Just as she

thought. There were two other listings. She phoned
both companies only to be informed that the only
thing they had in common with Penetti's Cab
Company was a listing in the yellow pages that
served two other small towns. They were both fifty
miles away and neither serviced Pine Mountain.

"Damn you, St. John," she howled. "Leave me
here without any way to get to town—without a
change of clothes. What am I supposed to do?"

She could wash her clothes and then walk to
town...if she knew the way. Why hadn't she paid
attention to how they'd gotten here last night?

Tess thumbed the thin phone book still in her lap.
At least she could call the fire department and find
out what conclusion they'd drawn about the fire at her
house.

Fifteen minutes later, she'd concluded her
conversation with the local Fire Chief. It hadn't been
Roman's cousin's cigar that had started the fire. That
news had dropped the floor out from under her. She
had only minimal insurance. Anticipating a speedy
turn-around on the house, she'd chanced saving
money by relying on her contractor's insurance for
protection.

Then came the reprieve she desperately needed.
The fire had started as the result of an over-heated
electrical cord Roman's cousin Raymond had
admitted to using.

At least those were the preliminary findings. The
Fire Marshall still had to investigate for himself and
write up his own report. But, with the only Fire
Marshall servicing all of Michigan's Upper Peninsula
gone on vacation, they'd have to wait for a downstate
Fire Marshall to fit them into his schedule. No rush
since there hadn't been any deaths or injuries as a

result of the fire. Apparently the entire Upper Peninsula was as remote as small town Pine Mountain.

Meanwhile, the Fire Chief had said she was free to *enter her property*. "Just don't go into the area where the fire occurred."

Don't go into the fire area? What kind of security was that? Roman and his henchmen could be at The Castle right now removing incriminating evidence. Could that be the reason he'd left her stranded, so he could get into the fire damaged area of The Castle before she did?

Tess paced the plaid and pine living room, debating whether the man who'd come with a sterling recommendation from her aunt—whether the man she'd come to know during long phone conversations would tamper with evidence. She picked up the photo of Roman's sister and nephew from the end table. Could a man who babysat a preschool nephew—who bought the boy a Winnie-the-Pooh nightlight for when he visited be so dishonest?

Being a good uncle to an adorable little boy didn't guarantee honesty.

She put the picture down and faced the fireplace that dominated the back wall of his living room. Made of fieldstone it created a handsome focal point for the room and certainly fit the rustic charm of the cabin. Okay, St. John had some design sense of his own.

She harrumphed. Having rustic taste didn't negate financial troubles, though. He sure wouldn't want to be found responsible for the fire at her place in that case. Then again, no contractor wants to be found at fault for a fire on his job.

That had to be his angle, remove all evidence his

crew was at fault for the fire. All men had angles. And St. John had plenty…like the angles planing his cheeks.

She groaned and began searching the collection of photos on the fireplace mantle as though she might find motive among them. There was a five by seven of a long-haired, young man with Roman's coloring and features dressed in knight's regalia and standing in front of two horses. The younger man had a wide grin and lively eyes. Another was of a younger Dixie in Dutch attire complete with wooden shoes, her pose flirtatious in a girlish way, her eyes inviting the viewer to join in her fun. An eight by ten landscape captured four blond-haired, blue-eyed teens in ski clothes on a snow covered mountainside, cheeks wind reddened. Siblings, no doubt. Something in the background reminded her of the Alps, but that couldn't be. World traveler just didn't fit her impression of Roman.

She picked up a photo of the four blond siblings with a fifth, dark haired boy all in orange cold weather gear on a background of snow. They were all a tad younger in this shot, the boys down on one knee with Dixie stretched out on her side on their upraised knees while behind them stood an older couple. Their parents, judging by the eye color the blonde siblings shared with the man and smile all five youths shared with the woman. And that smile wasn't just for the camera. Genuine happiness shown in their eyes, even those of the oldest looking boy with the dark hair and dark eyes.

Who were these people who appeared so open and guileless? Had Roman retained the honesty she saw in his younger self and of those he grew up with?

She needed to hash this all out with someone. If

only Aunt Honey weren't incommunicado. She could talk to Kitt who lived across the street from The Castle, the young mother she'd hired to help her clean out The Castle and pick through Honey's cast offs. They'd formed a close bond over a like-minded work ethic, their individual man troubles, and a shared appreciation for her contractor's physique.

But she didn't want to impose her issues on Kitt whose priority challenged husband left her short on funds for bills most months. Besides, she knew what Aunt Honey would tell her. The Fire Chief had already found the contractor's equipment to be at fault for the fire. There'd be no reason for Roman to remove evidence now.

And hadn't he already accepted responsibility? Honesty personified. Add reliable, neat, clean, and physically fit. He was damned near a Boy Scout. She needn't be worrying about him and his access to The Castle. Her worries should be focused on how to get The Castle cleaned up, repaired, and sold before her balloon payment was due.

"I need coffee." Tess charged the kitchen. A charred remnant of toast crunched under her foot, releasing new scorch fumes into the air and stopping her dead in her tracks.

Last evening, jogging the hilly neighborhood where The Castle held court, she'd smelled the smoke. Being an old neighborhood full of aged shade trees, she'd thought someone was burning pruned branches. Green wood burning would have explained the smoke plume spiraling into the sky.

But the childhood campfires and college bonfires of her youth had had a pleasant scent. This one did not.

The fire truck siren that had moments before

turned the heads of the small town folk but not that of a city girl suddenly took on an importance to her. The hairs at the nape of her neck had stood on end and she'd picked up her pace when she should have been slowing—cooling down. Each stride brought her closer to the smoke and hammered foreboding up her spine. By the time she rounded the last corner before The Castle, her muscles were burning.

Just like her house. Her one hope to prove her father wrong—to prove she could succeed on her own without him or any man—going up in flames.

"Thank you, Roman St. John."

Tess frowned at the mess her burnt toast had made of Roman's floor. Would serve him right if she didn't clean up. After all, if not for his defective equipment, her house wouldn't have caught on fire. If not for the fire, she wouldn't have been forced to move into *his* house. And if Roman hadn't abandoned her—hadn't left her to make her own breakfast, there wouldn't be burnt toast on his kitchen floor right now. She'd even had to sacrifice her first cup of coffee putting out the flames.

In her rebellious pique, she opted for making herself a fresh pot of coffee first. While it brewed, she went around opening windows to air out the place. After all, she was the one who'd have to breathe the fumes all day if she didn't. To get to the window in Roman's bedroom she had to go around his bed—his massive four-poster that screamed 'marriage bed'.

She skirted the big bed, eyeing it as she headed for the door. There wasn't so much as a wrinkle in its cover. Tess snorted. She'd bet Roman even folded his underwear.

She paused by the dresser and opened a drawer. Sure enough. His shorts were folded into tight little squares. She shook her head. "You're going to make some neat-nick woman very happy, St. John."

Of course, it wouldn't be her. She wasn't neat.

She wasn't husband hunting either. She was just a woman snooping through a man's underwear drawer, a very virile man's underwear drawer.

Neat or not, St. John was a man's man.

And not just because he wore plaid shirts, a hard hat, and a tool belt. He had a physique sculpted by physical labor and an ass made for his carpenter jeans.

Closing the drawer, Tess mewed in contentment. The marriage bed loomed before her and her mew turned to a resigned sigh. There could never be anything between her and Roman in the bedroom save for smoldering sex. Too bad because he really wasn't such a bad guy, judging by their phone conversations that had often wandered away from the job at hand into areas of general architecture. He was compassionate and generous, traits she'd witness one afternoon after he'd sent his crew home and he stayed to build new porch steps for the very elderly Mrs. Antonetti across the alley. Then there was the way he always managed to make Kitt's infant daughter smile by making silly faces or cooing at her.

She sighed. He was a natural with kids, not that paternal talents were even on her radar screen when vetting men. Still, he was a nice guy—a good guy. The fire at her house was an accident and no reason to leave his kitchen a mess. Just as it wasn't his fault all she and Roman could share was a fondness for similar architecture, steamy sex, and that they both liked to read in bed.

She fingered the reading material piled high on his nightstand. There were magazines dedicated to renovating older homes and a fat volume on building codes. And then there was that thin little book he'd been reading last night when she'd come to him for a nightlight, the one with the faded title he'd said was about a woman like her. She picked up the book and turned it over in her hand.

"Shakespeare. I'm impressed, St. John," she murmured as she squinted to read the faded title. But impressed wasn't the word that came to mind once she made out the words. *The Taming of the Shrew.*

He'd compared her to a shrew! How *dare* he? And after all the hassle and headache he'd caused her!

"Arrogant oaf." She slammed the book down on the nightstand.

"Pompous, patronizing neat freak!" she growled at the dresser with its drawer of precisely folded underwear.

"Condescending Cro-Magnon," she howled, hammering wrinkles into Roman's bedspread. "You think I'm a shrew? You haven't begun to see how shrewish I can be and to start with, you can clean your own kitchen!"

She stormed out of the bedroom in search of something to write on. "Let it never be said of Theresa Louise Abbot that she didn't give a man exactly what he deserved."

She snatched up the sticky note pad, but quickly discarded it. The yellow square was far too small for all she had to say to her contractor. Remembering he had an office, she raced up the stairs and into the room across the hall from the guest bedroom. She headed straight to the desk wedged in under the eaves, snatched a pen from a racquetball can next to the computer, a sheet of paper from the storage shelf beneath the inkjet printer and started to write.

Dear Mr. St. John:

No. Too polite.

Roman St. John didn't deserve polite. She crumpled up the sheet of typing paper, tossed it over her shoulder, and snagged another.

Look here, St. John!

The paper tore beneath the ferocity of her exclamation point. She balled up the paper and sent it after the first, snatched up another, and set pen to page. This time, the pen left nothing but scratchy little lines and faint dashes where letters should be.

Scowling, Tess dug in the racquetball tin for another pen. But all she came up with were pencils. No pencil lead would stand up to her writing. Not today.

She opened the top drawer of the desk and retrieved a fresh pen. Now, what to write?

She stared at the orderly surface of the desk. Computer, printer, scanner, mouse with mouse pad, racquetball can pencil holder, bills lined up in a file holder and books squarely braced between a set of pewter bookends. A place for everything and everything in its place. She was beginning to hate orderliness.

She swiveled in the chair, scanning the rest of the room. Identical in layout to the cozy bedroom where she'd slept, it was crowded, but organized. Pencils, erasers, and slide rule stationed on a drafting table in front of the dormered window overlooking the back yard. Wastebasket and low storage shelves lined up beneath the sloping wall like a preplanned subdivision of identical middle-income housing. Two filing cabinets flanked the doorway, not unlike a well-appointed entry to a grand estate. Even his contractor's license and a photo of a big old farmhouse hung above the desk as level as any well-built house's foundation.

But no college degree. No awards. Such certificates and plaques plastered her father's office walls. Yet Roman St. John was a building contractor who'd come with the highest of recommendations. Well-earned recommendation, judging by the work he'd done for her before the fire. No moneyed parents backing him, near as she could tell. Just a business built by the man's own blood and sweat.

"No, no, no," she muttered. "I am not going soft on him. He's simply a less educated version of my father. And he called me a shrew, albeit implied. He must pay, and with far worse than a mere scathing letter."

She stared at Roman's computer. Oh yes, there was much worse she could do to him than call him a few choice words.

She booted up his computer. There were any number of files she could mess up, provided they weren't password protected.

She tried one and smiled when it flashed open. "Oh St. John, you trusting fool."

She perused his accounting ledger, his quarterly profit and loss statement, and his estimate sheets. He could have charged his customers more, but he still made an ample personal income. A major portion of which he saved, she noted as she snooped further. More browsing and she amended *saved* with *invested.*

A man with security on his mind. She wasn't surprised. He was a man with his eye on a future that included a wife and children. A family man. He'd called himself just that many times while they worked together.

As much as that designation smacked of her

father, she couldn't make herself mess with the financial accounts of a man carving out a life for a family. Besides, any numbers she changed today wouldn't likely be noticed until tax time and she wanted immediate payback.

Tess closed the financial accounts and searched Roman's device manager for something more to her liking. She could alter his calendar where he'd listed all his jobs, but he also recorded his appointments in the day planner he carried with him. The man excelled at organizational skills.

She could mess with his program files. But, did she really want to do him irreversible harm?

But, he'd argued endlessly with her over the renovation of *her* house. He'd left her stuck in the boonies.

And he'd all but called her a shrew.

She could change the date on his computer.

Too juvenile.

But she was miffed. Hell, she was mad.

She opened his word processing program without finding so much as single letter. No personal journal. His emails were full of family correspondence, though. Nothing elaborate. Just short notes. Keeping in touch sort of things. Nice, that he kept in close touch with his siblings and parents. She moved on…and found his CAD program.

"Pay dirt."

Tess' fingers flew over the keyboard, opening files, scanning pages of schematic drawings. It was an earlier, simpler version of the drafting program she'd worked with at her father's firm, but familiar enough to her.

She studied a meticulously drawn electrical layout. But it wasn't Roman's neatness that impressed her now. He'd laid out a complicated routing as efficiently as any licensed electrician. No wonder he'd stuck his nose into the argument she'd had with the electrician rewiring The Castle and, to her astonishment, supported her point. He actually knew his stuff. Still, later, privately, she'd informed Roman she could handle her own disputes...even though it had taken Roman's intervention—a man's intervention to make the electrician do the job to her specifications.

Nice to have someone at your side to lean on now and then.

But also galling to need a man in order to get another man to listen to what she wanted. Besides, he was probably just showing off.

She pulled up another set of files. These included layouts for additions and garages, as well as floor plans to houses, and one labeled Dixie's restaurant kitchen. Curious, she opened the file. The blueprint depicted a commercial kitchen that was both functional and compact. Commercial building was far more complicated than residential mostly because of codes. Add that Roman had had to build the restaurant kitchen onto an old farmhouse...

Tess studied the farmhouse photo above the desk. She could see exactly where he'd added the kitchen. He hadn't charged his sister for labor, either. There hadn't been anything in his statements referencing any commercial properties.

She smiled. Family was supposed to support family and that was a good thing. Too bad her family never got the memo.

Her smile faded and she exited the file. One labeled The Castle caught her eye and she opened it. She wasn't surprised to see floor plans of her house, being he'd been the highest bidder on the property until she'd come along. She studied his plans. Other than giving the ground level a slightly more open floor plan and modernized kitchen, he'd made only minor alterations to the lower two floors. The big changes on his plan were to the attic, the third floor. A huge playroom dominated the space. It was a great use of the space for someone planning to raise a brood of children in that house.

In comparison, she had wanted it for an investment, her design marrying modern day convenience with yesteryear's grandeur, the emphasis on elegant living and entertaining space for the professional-minded. Not exactly what an old fashioned family man had in mind. Her design priced the house right out of a small contractor's price range, too.

Correction. Make that *would have* priced it out of Roman's range. She could forget about her prospective upscale buyers now that The Castle was a smoky, water-logged ruin.

Could that be Roman's angle? Could—would he have damaged the house so he could buy it at salvage price?

It didn't make sense. He'd done too much work on it already. Besides, he couldn't have predicted how much the fire would damage and he respected the house too much to destroy it.

But, even without ulterior motives, he'd still cost her the first entry into her architect's portfolio as an independent. Left her without a project with which to show her father she didn't need to play the *supportive little woman* to any husband in order to be successful.

"Damn you, St. John."

She considered tinkering with the CAD program,

replacing his plans with hers. It would ruin hours of his work...if he even needed it anymore. The house may be beyond repair. Or he may not be interested in taking on such a large restoration project.

As for restoring the property for her... Even if the house was salvageable, St. John Contracting wouldn't be awarded the renovation job, just the bill for rebuilding.

Regret shivered through Tess and she wasn't sure why.

Wrong. She knew exactly why, and it had nothing to do with an investment reduced to ashes and a lawsuit. There'd be no more contact with the man...except maybe in court.

"St. John, you are costing me big time grief."

CHAPTER FOUR

Roman gripped the truck's steering wheel, scowling as the truck trundled toward home. Today had nearly rivaled yesterday for worst day of his life, and not because the humidity level had turned an unseasonable warm spring day sauna-like.

He'd moved the crew to a new job site. But the building center hadn't delivered the necessary materials. By the time he had straightened out the mix-up and gotten the materials delivered, he also had three over-caffeinated employees. He didn't even want to think what that hour-long coffee break cost him.

Then he'd phoned the Fire Chief and gotten his preliminary findings regarding the fire at The Castle. It was little consolation to learn Raymond's cigar wasn't the cause of setting Tess Abbot's walk-up attic with its sheet-draped dusty boxes and tinder-dry antique furniture on fire, but that one of his electrical extension cords was.

While the boys took their lunch break, he'd headed over to The Castle. He'd expected to see Tess there and thought they might discuss her current living arrangement and how they might change it. But she wasn't there and her car still was.

He'd eaten his lunch there and waited. He'd waited until he ran out of time, something Tess Abbot apparently had an abundance of. Money, too, if she cared so little about additional damage standing water would do to her floors. Not that she considered any damage to The Castle her problem as long as he was responsible for the fire.

Looked like it was up to him to prevent further damage. He called his friends with the water extraction equipment, begged them to set aside their afternoon cleaning job and make The Castle a priority.

Then, just as the workday was winding down, Cousin Raymond runs a skill saw up his thumb. Two hours of hospital coffee and Roman had a caffeine buzz of his own that could have lit up Tess Abbots' beloved Chicago. At least Ray's thumb would heal, provided he didn't mind missing half a fingernail.

By the time Roman had secured the building site for the night and boarded up The Castle entry, he'd crashed from his caffeine high. But his head still felt as though someone was tightening a vice around it. Could this day get any worse?

#

The second Tess heard the rumble of a truck in the driveway she dropped the broom and ran to the front door. Forget the burnt toast crumbs, Roman was home. At least she hoped it was Roman's truck behind the blinding headlights and Roman inside it.

Anger had goaded her into invading his privacy, eating his pantry bare, and leaving the mess for him to clean up. It was the least she owed him. Or so she'd rationalized during her fits of temper.

But, as day faded into evening and he didn't return, her curses metamorphosed into concern. Maybe the reason he hadn't phoned to tell her he'd be late was because he'd had an accident on the way home. Or maybe he couldn't get through because she'd been on the Internet all afternoon vetting renovation companies that could repair The Castle. It wasn't her fault he lived so far out in the boonies he was still on dial-up service.

When she had realized how late it had gotten and she called his Cousin Raymond's number, the only other St. John listed in the phone book, she'd gotten some cocky kid who said they were all at the hospital and he didn't know anything else. The Hospital!

She called the hospital and been told no one by the name of St. John had been admitted. The ER department refused to give her any information since she wasn't a relative. She should have lied and said she was his sister or something. At least she'd have some information to assuage her concern, not that she could do anything to help him. Cleaning up the kitchen at least provided her some distraction while keeping her close to the phone in case someone might think to call her with information about an injured Roman.

Finally, the truck door opened and the interior light revealed a set of broad shoulders that could belong only to Roman. Tess let out a relieved breath. He appeared in one piece.

Halfway to the house, he bent and plucked the smoke detector off the ground. Tess winced. Here he might be hurt and she'd left his house a mess the better part of the day because of her stupid anger.

She slipped the dishes into the sink and squared the toaster on the back of the counter. The front door opened and Roman stepped in, frowning at the blipping smoke detector in his hand. The hell with dirty dishes. He could be stitched together somewhere.

She moved around the table toward him, noting he still had a mouth, a nose, and two complete sets of eyes and eyebrows in perfect order. He, on the other hand, looked at the wires hanging from the hall ceiling where his smoke detector had formerly been anchored then at the broom and the burnt toast remnants at his feet.

"What the hell is this, your version of payback? I burn your house, so you set fire to mine?"

Wasn't that nice? Here she was, worried about him, and what did she get for all her concern? Criticism.

Tess stopped dead in her tracks in front of Roman and planted her hands on her hips. "I didn't do it on purpose."

"That's comforting. I'd hate to think I have a pyromaniac for a houseguest."

He slammed the smoke alarm down on the table and she jumped...then counted the fingers white knuckling the smoke detector against the tabletop. All five fingers accounted for. The other set was curled into a fist at his side. A fist. How dare *he* be angry when she was the one with the charbroiled house and no way to escape this wooded hell while he could have been languishing in the hospital?

"Look here, St. John," she shot. "Maybe if you hadn't stranded me in the boonies—"

"Boonies? Stranded?" He snorted. "I left you sleeping in a warm bed and—"

"You looked in on me while I slept?" A strangely pleasant sensation tickled her ribs.

"—And the phone number of the local cab company." He plucked the sticky note off the table and flapped it in her face. "Here."

She snatched the note from his fingers and flung it aside. "Their fleet of one is getting a new transmission."

"Is that *my* fault? Does that give you the right to

trash my home?" He squatted and swept the toast remnants into the dust pan.

"I didn't trash your house," she said, surveying the top of his head for bumps and stitches. "I made a bit of a mess. I'll clean it up later. Just drive me to town so I can get my car."

He reared up before her, the dust pan of blackened crumbs wafting their ominously smoky odor up between them. "You expect me to drive you to town...now?"

"Yes, now. I want my car and I want it tonight."

He shook his head and headed for the sink under which the garbage can was neatly tucked out of sight. "It's late. I'm hungry and I'm tired."

"And I've been stuck here all day." She trailed him, perusing the contours of his close fitting jeans for tears and dried blood.

"I noticed you didn't arrange for anyone to start cleaning up the fire damage at The Castle."

"You said you knew some people who did water extraction," she said.

He faced her and blinked. "I mentioned them but you never gave me the go-ahead to hire them."

"Wasn't it obvious?"

"You're so dead set against accepting help, how was I supposed to know?"

"So my vintage wood floors are still sitting in a stew of sooty water?"

"No." He turned to the cabinet door. "I called the company. They started on the house this afternoon."

"Good. Now take me to The Castle so I can get my car."

"Your keys inside the house?" he asked as he emptied the dust pan.

"Of course."

He nudged the cabinet door shut with a perfectly working knee and faced her once more. "It's dark and they've turned off the power to The Castle."

"I'll use a flashlight."

"A flashlight? With your phobia of the dark?"

"I don't have a phobia," she said with only the slightest of hitches to her voice. "I just don't like the dark."

He stared at her, unmoving.

"Then take me shopping," she said, breaking the scrutiny of those eyes. "I need clothes and toiletries."

He brushed past her to the closet where he stored his broom and dust pan, giving her a good chance to sniff for hospital antiseptic. "Get out of bed before noon tomorrow and I'll drive you to The Castle. You can pick up your car and shop all you want then."

She trailed after him. "I didn't sleep till noon. And I refuse to wait until tomorrow for a change of clothes. I've been in this shirt of yours twenty-four hours straight."

He opened the fridge, bent, and peered inside. "Looks like you cleaned out at least one thing today, Princess."

"Don't call me Princess," she muttered, distracted by his backside as he pushed condiment jars around on the refrigerator shelves. She'd admired that narrow hipped butt countless times during the renovation...and daydreamed even more often about cupping those buns—

He straightened and caught her staring. "What are you looking at?"

She blinked at him, feeling every bit the petty thief caught with her fingers in the cookie jar. If he didn't stop staring at her, the heat blossoming in her cheeks would turn into a full-blown blush; and, hell, she never blushed.

But she would now, if he kept looking at her the way he did…if she didn't answer him. Damned thing was, she couldn't think of anything to tell him but the truth.

"When you weren't home by dark, I called your fire-starting cousin's house looking for you. His son said you were at the hospital. I was looking you over for injuries," she said.

A smile ghosted across Roman's lips. "Why Princess, I wouldn't have figured you for the maternal type."

She let the Princess reference slide, this time. But, maternal? Her? Never in a million years, especially not where a contractor with a butt you could bounce a quarter off of was concerned.

Tess folded her arms across her chest and lifted her chin. "Don't get a swelled head over it, St. John. My only concern was that you might not have told anybody you'd left me here and I'd be stranded until Penetti's Cab Company repaired its *fleet*."

His smile faded and he turned back to the sink for a damp rag. "Naturally it's all about you."

She frowned. "So why were you at the ER?"

He squatted over the crumbs that had evaded being swept up and wiped them up. "Raymond cut himself."

"Not bad, I hope."

He glanced up at her. "Careful there, Princess. You almost sound like you care."

"I do care," she said. "I don't wish injury on anyone."

He rose and went to the sink. "He cut his thumb bad enough to need stitches."

"And you took him to the ER," she said, relief

replacing worry. "That's why you were there."

"Yeah," he said, rinsing off the cloth and draping it over the faucet.

"I'm sorry about Raymond but glad you're okay," she said.

He faced her. "You are, huh?"

There was something in his eyes, a probing look that made her feel like he was peering inside her. No man had ever looked at her like that before and she wasn't ready for any man, especially this one, to see too deeply into her. She blinked.

"Did you leave anything for me to eat?" he asked, moving to the cupboard beside the fridge.

Peering over his shoulder, she saw a smattering of canned and boxed goods on the shelves. She pointed at a rectangular box. "You've got macaroni and cheese there."

"For when my nephew visits," he said.

"You can't replace it if you eat it?"

"Come on," he said, heading for the door. "You want clothes and I want food."

#

"It's this or nothing, Princess," Roman said, the giant letters of The Bargain Mart glowing through the truck windshield and washing Tess' face in a hue blue as her funk. "I'm not driving across town to The Castle."

"Pine Mountain isn't Chicago," Tess said, sounding every bit as annoyed as she'd been when she found out his truck didn't have air conditioning. "Across town here can't be more than ten minutes."

"Get up earlier tomorrow and I'll take you to your car then. I'm too tired tonight."

"You weren't too tired to go through that drive-through for burgers and fries," she said.

"You weren't complaining when you were wolfing down that mega meal and malt you ordered and I paid for," he said.

She glowered at the boxy building in front of them. "This can't be the only place even in this burg of a town where I can buy a change of clothes."

"It's not," he said and she lifted a hopeful eye his way. "But it's the only place open this late where you can get clothing and stuff."

She huffed and released her seatbelt. "Then make like a gentleman and open my door."

He raised an eyebrow at her. "Open your door? I thought you were a diehard woman's libber?"

Her head snapped in his direction, her hair swinging around her head as if in exclamation. "Men who use women's lib as an excuse not to open a lady's door are clods who didn't open doors *before* women's lib."

He put his drink cup in the cup holder, opened his door, climbed down from the truck, traipsed around the front bumper, and opened her door. "Let it never be said I was a clod."

She rolled her eyes, exited the truck, and headed for the store. He headed back toward the driver's side of the truck.

"I need you with me, St. John," she called over her shoulder.

"What? The automatic doors don't open fast enough for you?"

She didn't slow down. She just held up her arms and kept marching toward the store, barking out, "Do you see a purse? No, you don't because my purse and credit cards are still in The Castle waaay across town."

He groaned and headed after her. So much for

the compassion she expressed toward him when she thought he'd been the ER patient. It hadn't occurred to him that her concern might be for her own ends.

Inside the Bargain Mart, she strutted past the shopping carts. Good. That had to mean they wouldn't be here long. Right?

She went straight for the clothing section and stopped at a rack of skimpy undergarments. She selected panties made of a slick looking fabric, their high cut leg openings trimmed with wide bands of lace. She tossed them at him with a flippant, "They aren't silk, but they'll do for now."

"Maybe if you took only one pair instead of three, they wouldn't be too heavy for you to carry," he said, fumbling to grip the panties by their hangers and keep his fingers out of them.

She gave him a smirk and moved on to a rack of filmy nightwear. The muscles low in his groin yanked. There was only one thing worse than lying in his bed thinking about her asleep in the room above his in his t-shirt, and that was thinking of her asleep in one of those frilly contraptions. It was going to be an even longer night tonight.

Correction. There was one thing worse. Thinking of her asleep in nothing at all. But right now, he needed to deal with the effect those lacy nighties she fingered were having on his deprived male parts.

He plucked a full-length nightgown from the clearance rack and held it up. "How about this one?"

She eyed the nightgown with distinct disdain. "Polyester may suit your type of woman, but it's not my style."

"What do you mean, *my type of woman*?"

"The marrying kind."

"As opposed to you?" he asked.

Her big brown eyes narrowed at him, almost wounded looking. Then she blinked and the sharp edge of her voice sliced through the air conditioned air between them.

"Yes, St. John. As opposed to a woman like me who chooses career over marriage—a woman who isn't about to hide her talents behind a husband's ego."

She flicked aside the slinky nightgown and moved on, grumbling, "Is it too much to ask for something in cotton?"

"How about your mouth wrapped up like a mummy's," he muttered under his breath.

By the time the fifteen minutes to closing announcement crackled over The Bargain Mart PA system, he was beginning to feel like an overloaded coat rack.

"Come on," he urged, "they're closing."

She held up two shorts and crop-top sets. "Which color best suits me?"

The pink set made him think of cotton candy...and about nibbling the sweet confection off her body.

"The gray set," he said.

She smiled slyly. "I think I'll take both. After all, it's not like *I'm* paying for them."

"I'm paying for basics," he called as she traipsed off toward the front of the store. "Just the basics."

She didn't answer. He hung one of the crop-top sets back on the rack, the gray one, and followed her. At least she was headed in the direction of the cash registers.

But she ducked into the cosmetics department. Shoulders drooping, he followed as she piled herbal this and pomegranate that onto the clothes in his arms.

"You don't need all this stuff," he said as he eyed the bottles and jars identified as deep cleansing lotions, skin softening creams, and pore tightening astringents.

"Trying to save money, St. John?"

"I could remind you that most people don't have trust funds to fall back on. I should point out that, in the real world, money doesn't grow on trees, and that I work hard for the dollars you are so cavalierly spending."

"*Cavalierly*?" She hitched one eyebrow onto her high, flawless brow.

"Besides—" He put his face close to her scrubbed clean one with its sun-kissed cheeks and bare, burnished lips. "You don't need that gunk. You're beautiful without it."

#

He'd called her cosmetics gunk. She'd concede that the products the discount store sold weren't the best.

But what had stayed with Tess long after she'd left Roman signing the credit card receipt at The Bargain Mart checkout wasn't the gunk part of his comment. Nor even his lecture about money. What she couldn't stop thinking about was that he'd called her beautiful...*without make-up*.

Now, back at his house, Tess lie on the lumpy bed in the bedroom above Roman's, the warm glow of the Winnie the Pooh nightlight casting soft shadows across the slanted ceiling. In the city, a woman didn't step outside without her face made-up. Hell, women in her circle didn't leave their bedroom suites without their noses powdered and lips lined, which was a chore for a woman like her who liked to jog in the mornings. She had to either apply make-up before *and* after jogging or sneak out of the house to avoid her mother's, "A lady does not appear in public in disarray."

Tess couldn't remember ever seeing her mother without the requisite helmet hair. She couldn't picture her father touching her mother's sprayed to brittle perfection hair, either.

Roman St. John, on the other hand, was a man who'd run his fingers through a woman's hair. Oh yeah. He'd thread his long, thick fingers through a woman's hair all right. Tess dozed off thinking how Roman could cup a woman's head in his broad palm and caress her from head to toe without giving a single thought to whether or not he mussed her hair. He'd probably enjoy mussing it.

If only she dared let the contractor with the bed big enough to share with a wife run his fingers through her hair.

#

It was the thump on the ceiling above his head that woke Roman.

Not the low peel of distant thunder. Not the wind whistling under the eaves, or even the branch of the hundred-year old Norway pine scraping the north side of the house. He really should prune that thing back.

He yawned and rolled over, too sleepy to give further thought to what had hit the floor in the bedroom above his. Even the flicker of lightning burning white between the slats of the window blinds elicited little more from him than a sleepy blink. But the yelp underscoring that flash sent him rolling for the light on his nightstand.

Click. Click. The switch turned between his finger and thumb, but no light came on. The power was out.

And, in the room above his, his unwanted houseguest shrieked.

Grabbing the flashlight from the nightstand drawer, he jumped out of bed, bolted up the steps, and charged Tess' bedroom door. But the door was already half open, his momentum sending it banging back against the inside wall and him tripping over something that cursed in a voice he knew too well. The next thing he knew, he was hitting the floor with an *oomph* and the flashlight was rolling under the bed.

He groaned. "You really like to hurt me, don't you, Princess?"

"You're the one who came charging in here without knocking," she groused from somewhere in the vicinity of the doorway.

He rolled onto one hip and located her in the teetering beam of the flashlight. She sat on the floor near the doorway, the door that had given too easily beneath his hand and banged against the inside wall now swinging halfway shut behind her. She was rubbing her shoulder, the slick fabric of a newly purchased camisole like a second skin across her abdomen.

…which revealed the irregular rise of her navel.

She had a ring in her belly button. He could see it outlined by the pale, thin fabric. A navel ring. He should be appalled, squeamish at the very least.

But he wasn't.

No. That hidden treasure teased him, made him want to touch the ridge it formed in the pliant fabric—to trace a fingertip along its semicircle and across Tess' pierced belly button. It made him want to taste the cool circlet with his tongue.

To taste *her*.

The muscles low in his groin gave a little yank. Tess Abbot would laugh her audacious ass off if she knew how much she tempted him.

He tipped onto his backside and drew a leg up in front of himself in case his misbehaving body revealed too much against the smiley face pajama bottoms.

"You okay?" he managed, thankfully without sounding like a man in lust.

"You ran over me. What do you think?"

Her cryptic tone took some of the edge off his desire. He leaned back against the brace of his arms and sighed. "I heard you scream. I came up here to see what was wrong."

"I didn't scream," she said. "I never scream."

"Okay. Fine. I heard a noise and came to investigate," he retorted. "What were you doing on the floor in the dark?"

"That ridiculous nightlight of yours burned out and I couldn't find the switch for the overhead so I opened the door so I'd at least have the hall light. Why'd you turn out the hall light?"

The words tumbled from her, not at all the usual Tess Abbot clipped phrasing, and her fingers worried the thin strap of the camisole. There was more than a fear of darkness going on here.

"I didn't turn it off," he said in answer to her question and raising one of his own. "How'd you end up on the floor in the first place?"

She looked away. "Thunder woke me and then... Lightning filled the room."

Given their relationship had deteriorated these past six weeks into sniping at one another, a smart-aleck comeback formed on the tip of his tongue. But, he bit it back, the hint of vulnerability to her words—

her body reminding him he never kicked an opponent when he or she was down. "So you hit the deck. Lots of people are freaked by lightning and for good reason. It can kill."

She glanced ever so briefly at him. "Just turn on the light and leave me alone."

"Can't do that, Princess."

Her fingers stilled on the narrow strap of the camisole and she glowered at him. "What's the matter St. John, fingers out of joint because I made you carry a few things through The Bargain Mart for me?" she asked, though without the usual sarcastic bite.

"My fingers work just fine," he said. *Among other things*, he silently added, acutely aware of how the camisole clung to the rise and fall of her breasts, its clingy fabric molding to the dark, pebbled tips of her breasts.

"The power is out," he finished on a tight breath.

Apprehension flickered across her eyes as she glanced around the mostly dark room. "In that case, you can leave but the flashlight stays."

"If you're thinking of leaving the flashlight on all night," he said, "forget it. The batteries won't last."

"Ooh," she simpered, any sign of vulnerability shuttered away. "Should the frail, little woman beg the big strong man to stay and protect her?"

"Heaven forbid that you have to depend on any man," he said.

She blinked, her gaze not quite coming back up to his.

"I have a kerosene lantern downstairs," he said, reading an unease in the way she avoided looking at him. "I'll get it for you."

She hugged her knees up against her chest, that utterly feminine chest he'd already mapped with his eyes. "Fine."

"Stay put," he ordered, levering himself onto his feet, trying to figure out what it was about the way she hugged herself that didn't quite add up to the stubborn Tess he'd come to know. "I wouldn't want to trip over you again."

"Just go get the lantern, St. John."

He sighed and took a step toward the door just as a volley of thunder punched the air. Tess skidded backwards on her butt into the door with such force the door slammed shut. He stopped in front of her.

"You're going to have to move in order for me to leave."

"Okay," she said, but didn't move.

Near panic gnawed at Tess' gut as she stared into the blackness that defined the window. Another lightning flash turned the pines behind the house into a black picket fence, their pointed tops irregular—menacing. They'd taken her back to a nightmare of a night long ago.

"Don't like storms, huh, Princess?" If only Roman's voice had maintained the bite of his earlier words, there'd have been nothing to resist. But his voice had softened.

Heaven forbid that you have to depend on any man.

And wasn't he exactly the kind of man a woman could lean on. Reliable. But she wasn't the kind of woman who wanted to lean on any man. Still…

"Stay," she whispered, her voice raspy…thin. "Just until the storm passes."

His fingers twitched at his sides. "It can't hurt you here in the house, Princess."

Thunder rumbled through the house—through Tess. She shivered.

"Princess?"

Why did he have to keep calling her Princess? Why did he have to make this so hard for her?

Why couldn't she just blow him off like she did every other man?

A man to depend on—to lean on.

Tess shook her head, looked up at Roman, and muttered, "I'm going to have to tell you how I came to fear the dark and storms and everything that goes with them in order to get you to stay, aren't I?"

"Only if you want to."

She'd never told anyone the whole story. She didn't know if she could even now. If only she could see his expression—see if he taunted her, but his back was to the beam of the flashlight. Then again, he had left the choice to tell or not to her. She cleared her throat.

"I was at summer camp. Thirteen going on thirty. One of those posh places built on the bank of a private lake. Girls on one side. Boys on the other."

She paused, waiting for some snide reference to her privileged background—half hoping he would say something so she could stop before she made a total fool of herself. But he said nothing and she continued.

"I had a crush on one of the boys," she rushed out. "He snuck out one night, stole a boat, and sailed across the lake. I was waiting for him. We were out in the middle of the lake when the wind kicked up and the sails tangled."

The memory came back to Tess with an intensity she wasn't prepared for. She closed her eyes and was instantly back on that tiny boat in the middle of that night-blackened lake.

"The waves were wicked bad," she said. "We scrambled to straighten out the sails but…"

The words tangled in her throat. The silence stretched, then…

"Tess?"

A world of concern sounded in the voice that spoke her name. But she'd learned the hard way how superficial a man's concern could be. Yet, when she opened her eyes, there he was, hunkered down in front of her, a reassuring energy reaching out to her—his energy.

"It wasn't just wind, was it?" he said in a low voice.

She answered him in spite of her fear of revealing her weakness, her voice quavering. "It was a storm. The thunder so loud I couldn't hear what he was shouting."

"Something else happened, didn't it?" he said, drawing her further into that night.

Silently, she cursed Roman for probing—for making her want to tell the whole story.

"Yeah," she shot back at him, trying to hide behind her clipped city demeanor. "The boom hit me across the back and knocked me into the water. My little boyfriend panicked and sailed off."

Horror she expected to hear in Roman's voice, not anger. "Son of a bitch. How did you—"

"I swam," she cut in, afraid anything he said at this moment would undo her. "The storm woke my bunkmate. She knew where I'd gone. Knew the trouble I'd be in if I was caught. She found me…" *found me in a fetal position on the shore.* "She found me cold and exhausted and got me into a hot shower then bed."

"Hope the jerk got what he deserved," Roman growled.

The haunting fear melted at his words. That he

cared enough to be angry for her touched her deeper than anything any other man had ever said to or done for her. He made it tempting to accept his comfort, so very tempting.

"I didn't report the incident."

His head backlit by the flashlight, she couldn't see what was in his eyes, but she could see the hinge of his jaw pop. If she had any doubts what he was thinking, they were confirmed by his words.

"That means the little jerk didn't tell anyone you were out in the middle of the lake in a storm possibly drowning. That's criminal."

Her chest ached with a longing she didn't want to explore. She lifted a small smile at Roman.

"If I'd reported our being out on the lake that night, I'd have been the one expelled. I was a bit of a rabble rouser."

"You?" he said, mock shock tempering his anger. "A rabble rouser? I don't believe it."

"He's running for Congress," she said. "Maybe I'll volunteer to help his opponent."

Roman dropped down beside her, his back to the door, his shoulder touching hers. "That would make him sweat."

The kind of man a woman could lean on.

She wanted to lean on him. To give in to her desires for all the ways she wanted him.

And why not?

She was up on her knees, her lips brushing his before Roman even registered her movement.

"Thank you," she said, her breath a whisper against his lips.

"For what?" he asked, his arm automatically encircling her waist.

"For listening. For caring."

The thin camisole strap slipped off her bare shoulder. He shouldn't have put his arm around her. He'd realized his mistake when she leaned in for another kiss and placed her hand on his stomach just above the drawstring of the smiley face pajama bottoms. He covered it with his to keep her from venturing lower and discovering how his body reacted to her when all he'd meant to do was comfort her.

She shifted against him, one pebble hard nipple imprinting his ribs. The muscles across his abdomen bunched painfully. She edged a leg over his and that part of him most definitively male, that part hard-wired in antiquity to respond to the slightest call to procreate jerked.

"You could come downstairs with me while I get that lantern," he said, fighting the urge to slide his hand down that long leg hooked over his, to explore the sensitive back of Tess Abbot's knee and close his fingers around her slim ankle.

"I could," she said, but didn't move.

"Princess—" His voice was huskier than he meant it to be.

She rose onto her knees, straddling his thigh, facing him with her hands on his chest. He twitched where she touched him, on his chest, and there between his legs. He caught her by the wrists, half expecting her to start swinging once she figured out what part of him bobbed against her leg.

But she didn't swing. She didn't shrink away.

She didn't laugh.

She simply slipped one hand from his grip, reached down between them, and laid her hand lightly upon that part of him that nudged her knee—that part governed by the most basic of instincts.

He jumped against her palm and murmured hoarsely, "This isn't a good idea."

"No, it isn't," she whispered against the corner of his mouth a millisecond before slanting her lips across his.

Weeks of restraint evaporated in the conflagration of that kiss, of tongue meeting tongue. His hands flew over her, scouting terrain he'd up until now dared only look upon, gauging the angle of her hips and breadth of her back. His fingers tripped across her ribs and climbed the ladder of her spine.

Her hands were like firebrands against his chest, his shoulders, the back of his neck. Her fingers as urgent in their exploration as his. Her need, poised over his thigh, as heady and musky as his. Her tongue as adept in its circling, thrusting duel as his.

He brought his hands down over her hips, anchoring her against his rock hard need. She was hot and moist against his thigh. Ready.

He rolled her to the floor beneath him, mouth to mouth, breast to chest, pelvis to pelvis. He swept a hand between them and across the second skin of the camisole. His fingers found the hard nub of a nipple.

He tugged on that furled bud, making it grow, making it strain. Making her cry out against his mouth.

Her hands caught hold of his head and, the next thing he knew, he was beneath her. She ground her pelvis into his. Pain. Pleasure. He groaned into her mouth.

His fingers found the bottom edge of the camisole and slid across skin hot as fire. He cupped her breasts, filling his palms with her firm flesh and hard nipples. She was a perfect fit.

Perfect.

She reared back from him, breaking the hold of her mouth on his—of his hands on her. She gathered the camisole up her torso, the flashlight beam slanting from beneath the bed casting a long shadow from the gleaming ring piercing her belly button.

The ring he had wanted to touch with his finger and his tongue…and still wanted to.

He froze in mid-reach as she peeled the camisole up over her breasts. Lightning cut through the curtainless window, detailing her curves, turning the tiny gold ring piercing her belly button silver, and burning her image into his brain.

He stopped breathing.

Static electricity sparked from her hair as she tore the garment away, sparked off her fingertips when she touched *his* nipples. Breath slammed into his lungs. Life-giving oxygen jolted through his body. Every muscle contracted.

Yet, she didn't stop. She tweaked his naked nipples into tight, little balls—tweaked them until they ached—until he bucked against her. Bucked and slipped his thumbs into the high cut leg openings of her panties. Now it was her muscles tightening beneath his touch, her gasps filling the ozone laden air, her body swaying in the illumination of the lightning.

He stroked lower, deeper and a long, low rumble climbed from her throat.

She rose, tugged the happy face pajama bottoms from him, and skimmed the French cut panties down her long, runner's legs. He gazed up at her, caught in the flashlight beam escaping from under the bed. He gazed up at the ring glinting from her belly button and at the dark triangular patch of hair between her legs. He gazed up at the promise of paradise.

For one agonizing, eternal second, he thought it might have been a dream, her erotic caresses, her heady responses…her hot, musky scent.

Or maybe that it was all over—that she'd had her fun with him. Or her revenge.

Then she re-deposited herself astride his lap.

That most sensitive of male flesh butted against that most moist of female parts. Hungrily, they took each other's mouths, touched each other's bodies, circled each other's desire. A little shift one way or the other by either of them and they'd begin the slippery slide to oblivion.

He hitched one hip upward and she broke from his mouth, panting, "Not without protection."

"Protection?" he panted back against her soft lips.

"Yeah," she breathed against the corner of his mouth. "You know. Condoms."

He went still beneath her, poised there on the brink of heaven, and croaked out, "I don't have any condoms."

She blinked at him. "What kind of bachelor are you that you don't have condoms?"

He winced. "I intended to abstain until Ms. Right came along."

She sat back on his thighs. "But, like most men…"

"You're a liberated woman, every bit as hot and ready as me," he fired back, irked that she'd called him on the promise he'd made to himself. "Don't you have any condoms?"

The next instant she was on her feet, towering over him in all her naked glory. God, she was beautiful. He twitched painfully.

"Hello," she howled, jamming her fists against

her hips. "Did you see me arrive here with an evening bag? Everything I own is burned up or locked up in the charred ruin of my house."

He closed his eyes and groaned. At least that voice deflated some of the pressure building in his groin.

"No raincoat, no shower," she sang. "No glove, no admission. No safety, no holster for your gun."

"I get the picture," he growled, waving her aside and climbing to his feet.

"Where are you going?" she demanded as he opened the door.

"I'm going to get the price of admission."

CHAPTER FIVE

Roman was right. She was every bit as hot and ready as he. Like a desire brought to boil then left all steamed up without a way to vent. That's the state Roman had left her in when he'd put on his jeans and t-shirt and blown out with the storm. That's the state *he'd* been in when he'd gone out in the middle of the night to search out protection in a town that rolled up its sidewalks promptly at 10:00p.m.

Tess paced back and forth between the kitchen and living room, the power back on. She hadn't liked hearing the reason why he didn't have protection on hand.

She turned away from the front of the house, the slick fabric of The Bargain Mart robe slipping across her thighs reminding her of his caresses.

She advanced on Roman's bedroom where reality faced her head on. That dominating piece of furniture shouting *Marriage Bed* told her what kind of bachelor Roman really was. Roman was the marrying kind.

And she wasn't.

Sweat trickled down Tess' spine. She fled the room—the bed that was both temptation and trap. Trap she understood. But temptation? Of what? To finish what they'd started on the floor upstairs? Or was she tempted by something else Roman represented—something that would trap her? She had to think this thing between them through before he returned.

Back at the front door, she pressed her forehead to the cool glass. She stared out into the blackness, into a night closed in by a storm that hadn't broken, but had instead passed, leaving in its wake a sticky humidity. If only the storm of hormones coursing her body would likewise pass.

They would have at least been sated had Roman had the proper protection. They'd have finished what they'd started and that would have been that.

Or not.

Maybe Roman *not* having condoms was a sign. Aunt Honey would have said it was. And it was a sign as bright as neon spelling out how badly she needed to rethink this whole thing before proceeding. It was her father's *I told you so* in giant, flashing letters.

It was a billboard broadcasting the fact that the man she lusted for sought a wife.

Tess groaned against the dark glass, knowing the ramifications of the mistake they'd already made. Knowing they couldn't make another deeper, more costly mistake.

Truck lights slanted across the driveway. Tess backed away from the door, cinched closed the front of the sateen robe, and sat on the kitchen chair at the end of the table furthest from the door. Cold chrome touched the backs of her thighs and she jerked back onto her feet.

She should have chosen a robe that covered more than a modicum of thigh and was closed with buttons rather than a slippery tie. She should have shooed him out of her room the minute he volunteered to get her that lantern.

She should have kept her hands to herself.

But she hadn't.

He came through the door like a bull, a hot,

sweaty, aroused bull. Dark circles of sweat plastered his t-shirt against his ribs and his chest. Sweat sheened his skin and made his hair cling in wavy rivulets against his forehead. There was an intensity in his eyes as he strode toward her. A purpose. A determination. She knew exactly what it was without even reading the label on the small box caught between his fingers. She spoke before he could take her in his arms, because, once he touched her, she would be lost.

"We made a mistake," she said.

The fingers banded about the box flexed and one end popped open revealing the foil wrapped packages within. She recalled the tension in those fingers as they'd traveled across her skin—recalled how her muscles had contracted and rippled beneath his exploration. She ached to feel those deft, callused fingers play across her naked skin again.

"We shouldn't make another mistake, Roman," she said as he stopped in front of her, so near her she had to crane her neck to see into his face.

The dark lashes whose tips burned a fiery gold beneath the kitchen's overhead light lowered at her and he growled, "I should have known you'd pull something like this."

"*Pull something like this?*" She squared her shoulders. "I didn't *pull* anything. I came to my senses and, if you think about it—" She poked him in the chest with her index finger. "—you will, too."

Roman wanted to close his hand around that jabbing finger, bring it to his lips, and draw it into his mouth. He wanted to suckle it as he had her nipples, as he would other, more intimate parts of her body...if she'd give him the chance.

But those lips that had slanted across his, that had

parted in invitation, now shaped words about him needing to *cool his jets*, *keep his fly zipped*, and *think with the head on his shoulders*. Duct tape. That's what he needed…for her mouth.

"My senses were just fine until you forced your way into my house," he said through gritted teeth when she finally took a breath.

"And I wouldn't be here if you hadn't burned down my house," she returned.

He grimaced. "It didn't burn down. Just part of it burned."

"How nice that you were able to observe that fact for yourself," she said, folding her arms across her breasts, brushing his chest with the satiny cuffs of the robe that barely covered her thighs. He wondered if she'd put her panties back on. Wondered, if he reached into the opening of her robe, would he find the woman he'd almost made love to on the floor of his spare bedroom still wet and ready? *God*, he could still smell her arousal.

"It's my place and I haven't even seen the damages," she wailed on, jolting him back to reality.

"And how is that my fault?" he countered, irritated, frustrated. "You could have gotten up and ridden into town with me this morning."

"If you hadn't set fire to my place and made me homeless, I wouldn't have been in the position to need a ride into town."

"Damn it, Tess. If you weren't so bloody stubborn, you wouldn't be in my house in your skimpy underwear wreaking havoc with my senses."

"*Skimpy* underwear? I'm lucky I have any underwear, no thanks to you."

"No thanks to me? Whose credit card paid for this?" He flicked the lapel of the robe with a forefinger. A mistake. The silky fabric slipped across the tops of her breasts. No camisole lace to catch on. Was she naked beneath the robe?

No, he didn't want to go there. Not if she was no longer in the mood.

She swatted his hand away. He grabbed her hand and crammed the box of condoms into her palm. "Here. You might as well take these…just in case there's some other poor soul you want to torment," he said, and walked away from her.

"I'm the tormented one here," she shouted at his back as he strode toward his bedroom, peeling the t-shirt from his hot, sticky body. "I'm the one who was left stranded here all day!"

He pivoted on the threshold to his room and looked at her. A mistake, looking at that leggy body wrapped up in that thigh-riding robe. It just made him want her all over again. Never mind that she irritated the hell out him. That she frustrated him with her unrelenting mouth…and sound reasoning. She was right. They'd made enough mistakes for one night.

Hell, they'd made enough mistakes to last them a lifetime. He really had to get her out from under his roof before she burrowed any further under his skin.

"I'll wake you when I get up tomorrow and drive you to your house. You can get your car, pick up your things, and drive yourself to a motel. Any motel. I don't care. Just as long as you're not in my house when I get home tomorrow night."

#

As Mourning Doves cooed their love song, a moat-like mist shimmered off the dewy grass and streams of sunlight broke through a sentry of pines to fall across The Castle tower. But it wasn't the idyllic veneer of mist, stone, and seemingly unscathed first and second stories Tess surveyed through the broad windshield of Roman's truck.

Sooty stains fanned upward from The Castle's third floor windows and streaked the shingled siding. The roofline to one side of the house was interrupted where flames had leapt into the sky two nights ago. Then there was the yellow tape draping her broad stone steps warning away any without authorization to enter and a sheet of plywood nailed up where once had been a massive, hand-carved, oak door. The Castle looked about as patched together as her nerves. Why did she have to go and get naked with the tall, strong, and most assuredly *not* silent Roman St. John? That last was what spurred her own wicked tongue to counter his every word and deed.

Wrong. What goaded her to fight him was that, somewhere deep inside her, she knew she was more attracted to him than she wanted to admit. Oh how her father would gloat if she fell for a man with baby-making on his mind.

Her father who was no closer to recognizing her self-sufficiency than he'd been the day she'd bawled her way into the world as a six pound thirteen ounce newborn. His third daughter. He'd wanted a son. She knew because, whenever his parents fought, her father always threw it up to her mother that, in three pregnancies, she had failed to provide him a son. The only thing her father wanted from her now was a son-in-law.

Tess' fingers flexed around the travel mug of tepid coffee she'd hugged against her chest as Roman had driven her into town. The essence of the man whose work-roughened hands had played her body like a finely tuned instrument last night now crowded in on her in the small cab of the truck. Her nerves were frayed, doing jumping jacks across her skin as though she'd drunk a mug of espresso. Maybe Roman had been right to evict her from his home.

Roman shifted on the seat next to her, stirring the air between them. "You waiting for me to open the door for you, Princess?"

Again with the princess. How she hated that. Tess wrinkled her nose at him and jerked on the passenger side door handle. "Don't trouble yourself helping me with anything, St. John. I got this."

"Remember what the Fire Chief said," he called after her as she dropped to the ground. "Stay out of the fire area until the Fire Marshal has had time to inspect it."

"I know what the Fire Chief said," she retorted and slammed the empty coffee mug down on the floor of the truck, closed the door with more force than necessary, and strode purposefully up to the house.

She tore away the yellow tape and climbed the broad stone steps to the sweeping stone porch. She tested the edge of the plywood nailed across her front door...if she even had a front door any longer. The plywood was securely anchored in place. She wouldn't get in this way without a crowbar and it would be a cold day in hell before she asked Roman to loan her any tool from that industrial sized toolbox in the back of his truck. Besides, there was always the back door...provided that too wasn't boarded up.

She descended the steps. *He* stayed in his truck, one elbow hooked casually through the open window. Clearly any notion to help her eluded the inconsiderate lummox. Not that she was asking for his help.

"Wound a man's ego by refusing to have sex with him and he pouts," she muttered under her breath as she headed toward the back of the house.

If that was a truck door she heard open and close, he was too late to make amends. Tess quickened her pace, determined she'd find her own way into the house.

The back door wasn't boarded up, but it was locked. And her keys were still inside. She thought again of Roman with his truck full of tools. How easy it would be for him to pry the plywood off her front door.

She muttered a curse, found a loose brick among those edging the flowerbeds, and returned to the back door. She didn't need his help.

It took her three blows to shatter the windowpane in the door. She was plucking jagged shards of glass from the frame when a deep voice rumbled from inside the house, "Get back from there before you cut yourself."

She glanced up to find Roman looking out at her, a crowbar in one hand. "You pried the plywood from the front door."

"It seemed the reasonable thing to do."

"Reasonable would have been you letting me know what the hell you were doing *before* I broke a window."

"Reasonable would have been you asking for help," he countered.

"Are we going to stand here all day arguing?"

He flicked the deadbolt and opened the door, warning, "Careful where you step. Looks like some doofus broke glass all over your back entryway."

"Very funny, St. John," she snapped, dropping the brick into his hand as she strutted past him into the kitchen.

He watched her walk away from him. He wanted

to strangle her. He wanted to staple her carping lips together.

He wanted to wrap her long legs around his waist and take up where they'd left off last night...*before* he'd gone condom hunting. Why hadn't he just dropped her off out front of The Castle like he'd planned and gone to his other job site? Why'd he feel compelled to wait around to make sure she got inside okay?

And why the hell did he still want to make love to her?

He knew the answer to the first two questions. He felt responsible for her being burned out of her house. But that last question... He didn't have an answer to that one, at least none he was ready to face.

He tossed the brick out the door and trailed her into the kitchen. She was squatted low, rummaging around under the sink, the bike shorts tight across her behind. Memory of that backside bare beneath his palms sawed through him.

He turned away from her and the memory of last night. A carton of milk sat open on the countertop beside the fridge. He picked it up, sniffed it, and recoiled. "Whew. That's rank."

"My housekeeping skills not up to your standards, St. John?" she asked, coming up behind him.

"If the spoiled milk fits."

She shoved a heavy-duty garbage bag into his hand. "Here, Mr. Neat. Make yourself happy and empty my fridge before its rotting contents ruin the appliance."

"I didn't plan on sticking around."

"I don't imagine you planned on burning my house down, either," trailed her words as she disappeared into the next room.

Roman grumbled, opened the refrigerator door, and began scooping the contents from the darkened shelves into the plastic bag. Being responsible for the fire that gutted Tess's top floor was the only thing keeping him from stuffing her into the garbage bag, too.

#

Tess strode through the butler's pantry, the formal dining room, and the front parlor, the commercial sized fans drying her floors drowning out her curses. Damn Roman for following her into the house. Damn the man his take charge attitude.

Damn him for noticing she'd forgotten to put away her milk before she'd gone out for her evening run the night of the fire.

"Damn him," she howled at her gaping front door. The door she'd opened to him a mere six weeks ago when he'd come to start the renovating job. The door they'd both admired that day for its aged beauty.

Tess stroked the exquisitely hand carved door hanging lopsided from one hinge, the other shattered from the woodwork, a casualty of equipment laden firemen rushing to extinguish the third floor blaze no doubt. The woodwork could be repaired and the door had survived nearly unscathed. It reminded her of Roman. Solid. Reliable. Crafted for the long haul.

Ironic that she should find the one man who could reduce her dreams to ashes at Aunt Honey's home; flamboyant Aunt Honey whose example had given Tess the strength to confront her father and leave the firm. Tess could still hear her father's 'the-old-lady's-gone-over-the-edge' tirade when he'd learned Honey had bought an antiquated house in a remote corner of an out of the way state because it was where her Bentley broke down. Like Aunt Honey, she wasn't about to let any man get in the way of her career dreams.

Tess sighed and climbed the grand stairway dividing the house, the new but no doubt water-logged carpeting having been stripped away. The smell of smoke permeated the air, scratching her throat. She'd mortgaged herself deep into debt in order to buy the old place; she had sacrificed six weeks of her life and her fingernails to sanding, varnishing, painting, and repapering.

On the second floor landing, a table and vase she and Honey had found on one of their antiquing forays had been trampled. Like the first floor, the second hummed with fans. A quick tour revealed none of the rooms had been spared the greasy film of soot. It coated furnishings, clung to drapes, and bedding. It stained the hall walls dark where the smoke had been forced down from the attic before finding escape through the burned out roof.

She was tempted to follow the funneling pattern of stains up to the third floor. She'd like to see if any of Aunt Honey's boxes of memorabilia, racks of costumes, or stored furniture had survived the fire. If it had been only Roman St. John barring her from the uppermost level of her house, she'd have gone up there in a heartbeat. No man ordered her about. But the yellow *Keep Out* tape reminded her that a higher authority than Roman barred her admittance.

Water damage in the master suite left the ceiling sagging over the bed and plaster had collapsed onto her desk and laptop. She brushed the plaster aside and lifted the dented lid of the computer. It didn't look good. Still, she packed it up in its travel case along with her cell phone and several soggy rolls of blueprints. Clothes and toiletries were the next priority.

The concentration of odor-trapping fabric in the walk-in closet made it impossible for her to spend much time in the enclosed space. Everything would have to be laundered. The task seemed overwhelming even if she enlisted her neighbor Kitt's help. There must be professionals she could hire to do the work, even in little Pine Mountain.

She folded a few blouses and her favorite linen slacks into a bag. She added a pair of dress shoes and dumped the drawer of her undies onto the bed for sorting.

Fortunately, her personal belongings consisted primarily of clothing. Everything else was still in her Chicago condo. After all, The Castle had been meant only as an investment that was to have provided her a fast turn around and showcase photos for a new portfolio.

No portfolio pictures now.

No return on her investment.

Tess picked up a puzzle box from the nightstand beside her bed. She had kept this piece close because its enigmatic construction had inspired her and Honey to create endless stories about its use. Like all of Aunt Honey's collected antiques and memorabilia on the lower floors, it was coated with a greasy film. Everything on the top floor was likely a pile of ashes. She should have hired a moving company and put everything in storage. But she'd wanted to go through it all before disposing of it; and there was the matter of expense. Moving everything to the center of the massive space herself so the crew could drywall the "bonus room" had seemed the most reasonable choice at the time.

Regret balled in Tess' throat. Maybe her father was right. Maybe women *were* sentimental fools.

"Like hell," Tess muttered, carefully setting the puzzle box back on the nightstand. Wanting to check out what if anything of Aunt Honey's attic storage had survived wasn't being sentimental. It was being a property owner who wanted to survey the damage done.

The hell with her father, the Boy Scout contractor, and any yellow *Keep Out* tape. She was entitled to see how much damage her house had suffered.

#

Roman had emptied the fresh food compartment of Tess' fridge, gone into her basement to her electrical box and pulled the breakers to the attic, then called the power company on his cell to reconnect the electrical service to The Castle. He'd even chitchatted with Mrs. Antonetti from across the alley when she brought over a casserole for Tess. Still, Tess hadn't come down from upstairs. If he wanted to get to his other job site today, it looked like he was going to have to search out Princess The-World-Waits-on-Me to let her know about the electricity.

Even before he saw the yellow tape across the third floor stairwell fluttering loose, he knew the breeze sliding over him wasn't from the numerous fans doing drying duty. Someone had opened the door at the top of attic stairs. Three guesses who it was and the first two didn't count.

He found Tess on the third floor, a trim silhouette in bike shorts and Bargain Mart tee framed by charred beams and backlit by blue sky. He knew what those gentle curves felt like beneath his hands now.

An involuntary groan rumbled up from his throat.

She spun toward him, her foot tangling in a pile of rubble. She stumbled backward into the shell of a towering hall rack constructed of wood and wrought iron. For a second, she seemed to have come to a safe landing on its seat. Then the charred front legs of the chair-rack snapped and the looming structure pitched forward, pinning Tess to the floor.

Roman bolted to her side. "You okay?"

One dark eye glittered out at him from a framework of iron coat hooks. "Sure, St. John. I'm just peachy. Would you mind getting this thing off me? I think it skewered me."

He hefted the rack off her and helped her to her feet.

"Where'd it get you?" he asked, scanning her back.

"The back of my shoulder," she said.

"Uhuh," he murmured, fingering the tear in her shirt.

"How bad is it?" she asked.

"You're not spurting blood."

"Thank you for your medical opinion, *Dr.* St. John."

"I suppose that means you want a second opinion and that you expect me to drive you to the hospitable for it."

"I need to go to the hospital?" she asked with some alarm.

"Only for your wounded ego," he muttered and clamped a hand over her shoulder, trying to hold her still while he explored the injury beneath the rip.

"Hcy," she huffed, squirming beneath his hand, creating enough friction between them to re-ignite the attic. "You're the one who brought up the hospital."

"Stand still so I can get a good look at the

injury," he commanded, tugging at the collar of her shirt.

"There. I'm standing still. What's your final verdict?"

He released her and straightened. "It's a scratch that even a monkey could clean and bandage."

"A monkey, huh?" He didn't like the way she canted her head at him as she turned, or the self-satisfied smile she gave him as she started for the steps. "Come on, St. John. Let's test your theory."

Tess had liked the feel of Roman's hands on her shoulders. She'd liked it way too much. Goading him to tend her injury was just frosting on her cake of retaliation. Unfortunately, it back fired. They were now bumping elbows and hips in the narrow aisle between the bathroom vanity and raised Jacuzzi of the master bath, the door closed behind them reducing the roar of the fans to a low drone. He stretched the ribbing of her shirt back from the nape of her neck.

"You trying to choke me, St. John?"

"I'm trying to get a better look at that scratch."

"Can't you do that without choking me?"

"Apparently not."

"Let go of me." She twisted out of his grip, grabbed the bottom of her shirt, and peeled it off over her head.

He raised his eyes to the ceiling.

"Like you didn't see me in a whole lot less than a sports bra last night," she said, instantly regretting the reference to that incident where close quarters, lightning, and hot bodies had conspired against her better judgment.

"I was trying to be a gentleman," he said, lowering his gaze to her—letting it slide down over her, checking every inch she'd bared to him. His pupils flared, turning his eyes a sexy smoke-blue.

"Just check the cut," she said, giving him her back and trying not to look at him in the mirror and failing miserably.

"How long since your last Tetanus shot?" he asked, studying her shoulder.

"Less than a year," she answered, sounding far too breathless.

He grunted.

"What's that grunt supposed to mean," she demanded, letting her ready defensiveness put the edge back into her voice.

"Nothing. Turn your back toward the window. I need to get more light on the cut."

"That grunt meant something," she insisted, shifting toward the window for him.

"Maybe it just means I was impressed that you're up to date on your shots." His fingers framed the cut and stretched the skin around it. She started, but not because his touch hurt.

"Up to date on my shots?" She huffed. "You make me sound like a dog that needs rabies tags."

That got a smile out of him. Something she really hadn't meant to do. He had way too nice a smile. It showed his straight, white teeth and animated his face in far too appealing a manner.

His eyes met hers in the mirror above the vanity and his smile faded. "You got something to clean this out with, something sealed and still sterile?"

She pulled a first aid kit from a drawer at her hip, announcing, "Brand new. Figured I'd better have a stock of bandages with a building crew hammering about."

"You bought this for me and my men?" he asked, accepting the kit from her. Briefly, both their fingers held the case and a charge tingled up from Tess' hand.

"Don't get a swelled head, St. John," she said, releasing the kit to him. "We princesses sometimes look out for the little people."

"Smart princess, to take care of her subjects."

He set the kit on the vanity top next to her hip and popped it open. She should say something in response to what he'd just said, especially since it sounded suspiciously like a compliment. But his long fingers stirring through the contents of the first aid kit beside her hip just wouldn't let her think of any smart comeback.

He selected a package of gauze pads and bobbed his chin toward the medicine cabinet above the sink. "You got any peroxide in there?"

She nodded and retrieved the bottle before he could reach for it himself. She didn't need him leaning any closer than he already was.

"Ready to test that theory about monkeys?" he asked, holding up a peroxide soaked gauze pad in his hand.

She met his bemused eyes in the mirror. "Just do it, St. John."

He dabbed at her shoulder with the pad. Cold liquid dribbled down her back and she arched away from him.

"You had your belly button pierced. This can't hurt worse than that," he said.

"I didn't jump because the peroxide burned. I jumped because it's cold and you dribbled it down my back."

"Ah." He dabbed her shoulder with a freshly doused pad, catching the excess this time with a dry pad. "Why'd you do it?"

"Do what?"

"Pierce your belly button."

"To aggravate my father."

"That was grown up of you."

Tess frowned. Roman was right. She'd done more than a few silly things in her youth to get her father's attention. No wonder the old man was certain she'd fail. He probably still saw her as that rebellious child motivated by all the wrong reasons.

She sighed. "A lot has changed since those days."

"Like what?" Roman asked, studying Tess' reflection in the vanity mirror.

Her gaze broke from his, the angle if her eyes seemingly fixed on the sink and she shrugged. "I grew up. Chose a career path."

Given the way she hugged the t-shirt to her stomach and puckered her brow, he'd bet dollars to doughnuts Tess Abbot had some unresolved father issues.

He spread an adhesive strip over the wound, wanting to know more but fighting the urge to press for more. Look where comforting this woman had taken them last night. It was a mistake he wouldn't make again.

"There," he said, removing his hands from her back, so far surviving the temptation she presented him. "Now all you have to do is stay out of places where you can get hurt."

"I was safe enough in the attic until you snuck up on me and startled me," she said, pulling the t-shirt on over her head.

Damn, but didn't he want to fit his hands around her…

She faced him and leaned back against the counter, her hands braced to the edge of the vanity on either side of her hips. It was a challenging pose that almost took his mind off how inviting her bare skin had been just before it disappeared beneath the t-shirt—almost made him forget how, only moments ago, her shoulders had curled protectively in on her. She'd had the same defensive look about her last night as she'd recited the details of her near drowning. Damn, but the woman confused him.

"I didn't sneak up on you," he said, wanting to comfort her and throttle her all at the same time.

"You came checking up on me," she accused.

He rolled the bandage wrapper into a tight ball between his fingers. "You obviously needed checking up on."

"Afraid I was going to tamper with evidence?"

He leaned in close to her in spite of the danger she presented. "Is that something I need to be concerned about with you, Princess?"

"No."

She didn't shrink from him. She didn't flinch. She didn't give an inch. And that single syllable word she'd spoken shaped her mouth into the most alluring circle.

He dropped the remaining gauze pads into the first aid kit, snapped its lid shut, and eased back from her. "I came up to tell you that I was leaving."

"Good-bye," she said with effusive joy.

"And that I pulled the power to the attic and called the electric company to reconnect you."

"I bet you were a Boy Scout when you were a kid, one of those boys with all the badges."

Roman bit back a retort, refusing to rise to her baiting. "I'll come by later with Ray and we'll tarp your roof."

"Should *I* be concerned about you crossing that yellow tape?"

"We won't need to get inside the house to do it."

"Uh huh."

"And one more thing. Mrs. Antonetti brought you a casserole."

Tess' face brightened and her defensive pose disappeared. "A casserole? From Mrs. Antonetti?"

"Yeah."

"She's a really good cook." Tess licked her lips.

"Prize winning," he murmured, distracted by the pink tip of her tongue sweeping across the cleft in her bottom lip.

She looked up at him and the brightness dimmed from her features. "You take the casserole. I won't have any way of heating it up in a motel room."

"Get a condo at the ski hill with a kitchen. Make that a kitchenette. No sense wasting a full kitchen on you."

She made a moue face. "Just because I had a little mishap in your kitchen—"

"You call nearly setting fire to my kitchen a mishap?"

"You didn't even suffer smoke damage. Take a whiff of my house."

He nodded. "You need an ionizer. The people I recommended with the water extraction equipment do air purification also. Shall I give them the go ahead or do you want to handle it?"

"Yeah. Tell them to take care of everything." She waved him out of her way, but paused with her hand on the doorknob. "Can you recommend a professional cleaner being you seem to know everyone in town? Every piece of clothing I have here reeks."

"Any of them will do a good job. But they're open only until noon today. It's Saturday."

"Another charm of Small Town USA. I'll be

lucky if I see my clothes by midweek."

"You could take them to the Laundromat yourself."

A shadow darkened her eyes. Before Roman could figure out what it meant, she opened the door and stepped out into the roar of the fans. But he could still her. "I have a hole in my roof big enough to drive a bulldozer through. I'm in no mood to sit around any Laundromat waiting for my underwear to dry."

Like the underwear piled on her bed no doubt. Silk scraps of lace trimmed and frothy colored.

The muscles in his groin cramped. She was *not* the woman for him. But it was his fault her house had nearly burned down...that her underwear was presently unwearable. He owed her. He sighed. He was going to regret this.

"Take your stuff back to my place and use my washer and dryer."

Her chin came up. "Is that an order, St. John?"

"It's an offer."

CHAPTER SIX

Tess stared at the alien appliances in Roman's bathroom closet. Oh, she knew what a washer and dryer were. She even knew what they did. What she wasn't well versed in was how to operate them.

Why then had she taken Roman up on his offer to do her laundry at his house?

Because of ego. She didn't want Roman to know her experience with washing machines and dryers didn't exceed single digits. A few forays to the Laundromat during her college days and the novelty of doing her own wash had worn off. She simply had better things to do with her time.

Except now. Right now, clean clothes were top priority. But how to accomplish the feat with a contraption that had entirely too many dials?

Did she use hot, cold, or warm water? Full capacity, small load, or somewhere in between? Gentle wash, regular, or heavy duty?

At least the detergent boxes gave directions. She just needed a couple hours to sit and read all the fine print.

Tess fingered the silk blouses and lingerie in the garbage bag. She gave her favorite linen slacks a nudge. Gentle wash for sure. They probably should not be washed in hot water, either.

But, did she put everything in all at once? Was Roman's extra strength laundry detergent too harsh for washable silk and linen? If she ruined her clothes, how long would it take for her favorite boutique to send replacements? She'd really had enough of the pretending-to-be-silk, Bargain Mart panties sticking currently to her butt.

She frowned at the appliances in the bathroom closet and hugged her bag of delicates protectively. If only she knew her way around a clothes washer as well as she did a drafting table. If only she hadn't been too embarrassed to confess to Roman her limitations as a laundress. If only she had some items made of hardier fabric to practice on.

Her gaze wandered to Roman's dirty laundry in the clothesbasket on top of the dryer. Jockey shorts, t-shirts, and towels. They certainly were made of sturdier stuff. Tess smiled. She could practice using the washer and dryer with those shorts, tees, and towels and, as a bonus, Roman would get clean laundry. If she put the load on heavy duty, she'd even have a nice long stretch of time to do some business via the web.

"Sounds like a winner to me," she chirped as she scooped the jockey shorts and t-shirts into the top loader and piled the bath towels on top of them.

The water temperature dial was already punched on hot. Seemed reasonable to her, at least for sturdy man-clothes.

"Maximum water level, heavy duty wash, and a cup of detergent. Just like riding a bike," she murmured, watching the steamy water pour over Roman's white shorts, navy tees, and burgundy towels.

#

It took an extra rinse cycle to get enough soap out of the towels and tees that they stopped producing suds in the rinse cycle. But even a third rinse didn't wash the pink tint out of Roman's jockey shorts.

Tess tucked the stack of pink underwear into Roman's dresser drawer under his last two pair of white ones. Maybe he wouldn't notice. They were a very pale shade of pink. Hardly noticeable...except next to the bright white shorts. Good thing she'd opted for hand washing her dirty clothes.

She smoothed the dazzling white underwear over the faintly pink shorts even though she knew her misguided laundering would not go unnoticed by her eagle-eyed host for long.

#

Roman had a dead cell phone battery and a headache that measured in at about five foot six named Tess Abbot. It seemed his houseguest had gone directly back to his house after leaving hers and planted herself on his phone. Apparently she had done the same thing yesterday as well, given the endless string of complaints he'd gotten through the afternoon from clients and potential clients who'd tracked him down via his cell phone. Every one of them told the same story. They hadn't been able to get through to his land-line to leave a message on his answering machine.

Whatever had possessed him to invite Tess Abbot back into his home?

Long legs, perfect palm-sized breasts, and a full bottom lip with a sexy cleft dead center. The answer wandered through his over-taxed brain.

No. No. No. He'd relented because she'd injured herself, she needed to wash her clothes, and all because he was responsible for the fire causing the damage. He owed her.

More like he'd been suckered in.

Roman took the turn into his driveway a tad tight and hit the pothole he'd affectionately named

Goodyear after it had blown one of Raymond's truck tires. The jostling that hole gave Roman, though, didn't evoke any humor today. It only rattled his already throbbing brain against his skull.

"For your sake, Tess Abbot, that phone had better be out of order."

He stormed into the house, barely glancing at her as she descended the steps. He went to the wall phone, lifted the receiver, listened, hung up, and turned on her. "It's not out of order."

She blinked. "Did you expect it to be?"

"From what my clients who've been calling me all day on my cell phone tell me, I expected it to be. That would be my clients and *potential* clients who've been trying to call and leave messages on my answering machine the past two days. Who the hell do you know around here well enough to spend all day on the phone talking to them?"

"I—"

"No. Don't tell me who. I don't care who you talk to. All I care about is that half the town of Pine Mountain now has my cell phone number and is using it to reach me."

She planted her hands on her hips and raised perfectly arched eyebrows at him. "And as a man who owns his own contracting business this is bad how?"

"With my cell phone ringing all day long, I don't get a lot of work done."

"Have you ever considered hiring office staff to answer your phone?"

"The answering machine was working just fine until you came along. Besides, even if I had an office staff, how were they going to answer a phone you were yapping on?"

"You know what your problem is, St. John?"

"I have a pampered princess tying up my phone?"

Through tight lips, Tess countered, "I am not a princess. I am not pampered. And I did not use your phone to entertain myself. I was making business calls."

"You have your cell phone back."

"Which took time to charge."

"That couldn't have taken all day."

"But Internet out here in the boonies—"

"You used my computer?"

"Hello, mine is waterlogged with a serious dent in its lid because there was a fire in my house that dropped a ceiling on it. And whose fault—"

The veins popped out in Roman's neck, enough so she went silent in mid-sentence.

"I do a lot of business via the Internet," she said.

He threw up his hands and stalked off down the hall, muttering, "I'm going to go and soak in the tub."

Mention of the bathroom reminded Tess of her laundering job, specifically his shorts and towels. She turned after him. "Roman—"

"I don't want to hear anything else from you tonight," he called over his shoulder.

"But I washed your shorts and bath towels."

"Bully for you."

"You don't understand. The towels are burgundy and the shorts white."

He stopped on the bathroom threshold and looked at her through narrowed eyes. "What? You want a medal for doing my wash, or a chest to pin it on?"

Tess folded her arms across her less than abundant chest. He had some nerve making a comment like that after the way he'd pawed her breasts and played torturous games with her nipples.

She advanced on him in the narrow hall between the stairs and the bathroom, chin held high. "I just—"

"—Wanted me to know you did something else besides tie up my phone all day? Fine. Now I know."

"But—"

"Peace and quiet. That's all I want."

"But—"

He pressed the side of his finger against her lips. "Not another sound. Not a peep."

He stepped into the bathroom and let out a god-awful groan. She moved into the doorway behind him and found him tearing her panties and bras off the shower rod, towel racks, and from over the open closet doors.

"Some of those aren't dry yet," she protested as he dumped them into her arms.

Holding up one shushing finger, he shut the door in her face.

To hell with Roman St. John. If he didn't want to hear her out, then let him find out on his own about his shorts. Infer that she needed a chest, would he? The next time he tried to cop a feel, he might just pull back a bloody stump.

#

The sunlight piercing the bedroom window hit Tess in the face. She blinked and bolted from the bed. She was halfway to the door before she remembered she didn't have to rely on Roman for a ride today. She had her own car.

She regarded the lumpy bed beckoning her. But decided her time would be better spent at The Castle itemizing what needed to be done to put the house back in order. She could start tossing out a few things that were beyond repair.

No. Wait. She couldn't go into The Castle. The place was being ionized today and that meant she couldn't go inside until Monday morning.

The bed was looking more inviting by the minute. Except, when she slept she dreamt of Roman and those dreams weren't sweet. More like triple X-rated.

She groaned and set about her morning ritual, selecting one of her skin lotions from the dresser top...the good skin lotion, not the one she'd picked up at The Bargain Mart. That stuff was gunk...just like Roman had said.

She grunted. Couldn't she even apply skin lotion without thinking of him? Maybe it was time she found a bed that wasn't upstairs of Roman's bedroom. Though, if she moved out, she wouldn't have Roman's computer at her disposal. And God knows how long it would take for the local computer company, the one and only computer repair shop in Pine Mountain, to repair her damaged laptop.

She scowled and spread a dollop of lotion up her arm. Whatever had she done in life to deserve this rural hell besides walk out on her father? A father who consigned his daughters to domesticity. A father who valued them only for the quality of sons-in-law they could attract into the family.

A father who'd betrayed her when he should have lauded her. She was a good architect. Why couldn't he accept that? Why did he have to treat every woman as if she had no more sense than a child?

Like Roman St. John who'd gone ballistic over his phone. She scrubbed lubricating lotion into her elbow. Here she'd washed his underwear and all he could do was rant about her tying up his phone.

She wasn't a child to be dressed down. That's

what she should have shouted back at him instead of trying to explain about his shorts.

A burning sensation radiated from her elbow. She stopped rubbing the perfumed skin cream into it, snapped the cap back on the tube of lotion, and examined her elbow in the dresser mirror. It was red...irritated from over stimulation...like her. That's what Roman did to her.

No wonder, by the time she'd found new places to spread out her drying undies and he was done with his bath, she no more wanted to talk to him than drive through a bad Chicago neighborhood at three a.m. with an empty gas tank. Lucky for him, he'd had the sense to not comment on the hamburgers she'd cooked...not even when they crunched.

Oh, no way was she moving out. She was nowhere near done punishing him.

She flung aside the tube of lotion and jerked opened the narrow top drawer where she'd put her underwear after it had dried. The box of condoms slid across the bottom of the drawer and butted up against her panties. An unexpected pang of desire surged through her. How easily she could end this aching frustration for both of them.

She fingered the condom box in her lingerie drawer...the *open* condom box. Some of the foil wrapped packets were missing. She'd checked. Where had Roman gone two nights ago to get that box of condoms? Not to a drug store. Drug stores didn't sell unsealed boxes of condoms with product missing. He'd have to have gone to a friend.

A friend.

So, Roman St. John had himself a friend he was close enough to that he could go to him in the middle of the night for a package of protection...when he was in dire need...when he had a woman ready and waiting. Not that she was all that surprised. He had a casual work relationship with his employees, judging by their overheard plans for "a beer after work" or the on-the-job teasing they exchanged. He was more than cordial with her neighbors, even flirting with the elderly Mrs. Antonetti.

So he was well-liked enough to sometimes head home at the end of the day with a plate of Mrs. Antonetti's ravioli or a cannoli or two. Mrs. Antonetti also gave her ravioli and cannoli. Then again, her sweet, old neighbor had called her and Roman the perfect couple when Roman had reinforced the lintel above her back door after Tess had diagnosed why it was sagging and causing her door to stick in wet weather.

The perfect couple. Tess shuddered. That's exactly why she had to ignore Roman's current frustrated state and her own. As long as she didn't want to be coupled with any man least of all one looking for a wife, abstaining was in both their best interests.

Though, clearly, Roman wasn't thinking about how their abstaining affected her. Wasn't that just like a man? Leave him a little frustrated and he acts like you castrated him. Like he's the only one suffering. The only one with urges. Needs.

Desires.

Dreams of love.

Tess groaned and shoved the box of condoms aside. She didn't have time for love. Not with her father breathing down her neck, waiting for her to fail. She had no time for Roman, real or fantasized. She would dress in her hand-washed silk panties and go for a run, which should clear her head of all this sexual temptation and enable her to think out a timeline for getting The Castle back up for sale. If she was lucky and worked fast, she might even get it back on the market and sold before the bank repossessed it.

Yep. A cup of coffee and a long run. That would get Roman out of her head.

#

The sweet tang of almonds wafted past Roman's nose. Tess had invaded his kitchen. The woman didn't cook, yet she wore…flavors. Vanilla, strawberry, almond. He must have worked for her two weeks before he'd figured out those scents had nothing to do with baking. That in itself should have warned him away from her. The future Mrs. Roman St. John should be a woman who smelled of flavors because she knew her way around a kitchen, right?

He dug his knuckles into the bread dough on the counter in front of him, kneading the dough and, hopefully, the tension from his shoulders. The fact that those enticing scents came from the bottles, jars, and tubes lined up on the dresser in his guest-bedroom should be a warning as pungent as a skunk that pretty little packages shouldn't always be invited into your home.

The Harridan Princess was in for a surprise if she thought the local populace had surrendered itself to her subjugation. If she thought for a moment he'd relent to this latest invasion of his space and let her stay, she was in for a big surprise.

She moved to the counter beside him. For all his determination, the assault of her nearness worked on him like yeast stirred into warm water. He punched the bread dough.

"That coffee still hot?" she asked, her little chin bobbing at the coffee maker on the back of the counter beside where he worked, her tone suspiciously congenial.

"Yeah."

She inclined her head toward the cupboard above him. "Think I could have a mug?"

"Help yourself."

"Gee, St. John, don't sprain a wrist getting a cup for me."

Finally, a tone he was familiar with.

She reached past him into the cupboard for the mug, her breast brushing his elbow. He should have gotten the mug out for her. He should have moved aside and given her room. But she had a knack for making him dig his heels in, for making him resist giving her so much as an inch of leeway.

It was a tactical error, pitting stubbornness against stubbornness. She was the Princess of Pig-headedness.

And he was the court fool, standing there suffering the contact of her curves as she reached around him for a coffee mug. He'd mapped those curves with his eyes, his hands…his mouth. He'd climbed their enticing slopes and free-fallen into their valleys. He'd been on the brink of the Promised Land only to be barred entrance.

He punched the bread dough again.

As she lifted the pot from its heating tray, he gave her a sidelong glance. Skin tight running shorts. Over-sized t-shirt knotted up at her waist. Sleep tousled hair and naked lips. Damn she looked sexy.

He took a travel mug from the cupboard and banged it down on the counter in front of her. "Here."

"A travel mug?" she asked, coffeepot poised over the stoneware mug she'd chosen. "Am I going somewhere?"

"To The Castle?" he said hopefully.

"Can't," she said, filling the stoneware mug. "It's being ionized today."

"Lucky me," he muttered and punched the bread dough yet again.

She jammed the coffeepot back onto its hotplate. "Look, St. John, I'm trying to be nice here."

"Haven't had much practice at it, have you?"

Her mouth popped open.

He flipped the dough over with such force it raised a cloud of flour.

She fanned the flour dust away from her mug. "Just because I rejected you the other night—"

"Rejected me?" He rounded on her. "Somebody here has an inflated ego and it's not me."

She snorted. "Get real, St. John."

He shook the lump of dough in her face. "I'll tell you what's real. Real was *you* stripping off my pajama bottoms. Real was *you* sliding *your* hand into my crotch. Real was *you* begging me to stay."

Something glinted in her eyes, something that made him think of…yearning. Or was it passion he saw in those dark depths? Or fight? Fight would make sense. More sense than the suggestion of fright he thought he glimpsed before she blinked away everything but her usual princess-like glare.

With the backs of two fingers, she pushed the lump of dough away from her face and raised the coffee mug toward her lips. "Must you rant on before I've even had my first cup of coffee?"

God, but she was maddening. And damned if he didn't want her more than ever because of it.

CHAPTER SEVEN

Sweat plastered the t-shirt to Tess' spine and dripped down her brow into her eyes. Her calves burned from running and her hands ached from clenching them into tight fists. She'd been running for an hour and hadn't had a single thought about The Castle. Too bad she couldn't say the same about Roman St. John. So much for clearing her head of that man.

If only he hadn't thrown the details of their aborted affair in her face, especially the detail about her stripping off his pajama bottoms. Oh those happy face pjs and the wonder of Roman St. John rising beneath them. How naturally her hand had—

"Don't go there," she panted, her feet pounding the blacktop road that wound through woods, over creeks, and past dirt driveways.

If only he wasn't such a blasted Boy Scout. Then she could have slept with the man, rid herself of this insane itch, and moved on with her life. But no, *he* had to be the one man she was attracted to, a blasted knight come to rescue the damsel in distress and, worse, marry her.

Why had she admitted her fear of the dark to him? Why had she told him about that damned stormy night when she'd almost drowned? She hated the damsel in distress thing. It made a woman seem weak and turned men into chest-pounding rescuers. And no man had ever helped her that didn't have an agenda of his own.

So, what was Roman's?

To get her out from under his roof. She couldn't very well blame him for wanting that. She'd insulted him, wounded him, and goaded him. And he didn't seem to have a motive beyond that...except to finish what they'd started two nights ago, something that tempted her to distraction as well. She really should move out.

But who would hold her through the next storm?

Tess scowled as the corner before Roman's place loomed closer. She didn't need a man to hold her hand through stormy weather. She'd dealt with wind and lightning on her own before, though she'd usually done so by closing her drapes, cranking the volume up on her CD player, and crawling under the covers in her Chicago condo.

Make this work for you, girl. Make leaving more attractive than staying. Yeah. I could go back to the city.

The city where she could be anonymous.

"Provided I don't run into my father, my jerk of an ex-fiancé, or anyone connected with either of them."

Where there were no neighbors like Mrs. Antonetti who brought her homemade apple pie and told her stories about Aunt Honey. Or Kitt Delaney, the young mother across the street, whom she'd hired to help her clean The Castle and whose company she enjoyed. Okay, so there were some good points to Pine Mountain.

But the city is convenient.

Except for parking shortages, traffic jams, and endless lines.

The city has plays, and art, and real people playing real music to real audiences, she silently lamented into the fresh country air, feeling a little nostalgic for bus exhaust.

Just then, a truck lurched around the corner, its rust-patched chrome bumper catching the sunlight and reflecting it back into her face. Its over-sized tires spit gravel as it veered momentarily off the blacktop. Tess was halfway into the ditch by the time the truck righted itself and sped off down the road, the cab full of teenagers laughing.

Muttering a curse, she climbed back onto the gravel shoulder of the road. The ball of her foot hurt when she took a step. She must have bruised it stepping on a rock on her way into the ditch. At least in the city there were no ditches to fall into...just curbs, which a person could rely on to be gravel free. Though there was the occasional wino.

Still, in the city, a person knew what to look out for. A person was safe there...at least from a well-muscled, protective Norse God of a man.

Tess limped around the bend towards Roman's house. She was done running. She was done debating. The bottom line, she was too attracted to the man to stay under the same roof with him. If she stayed, sooner or later, she'd lean on him for support again. Let him support her in any way, shape, or form and her father would consider her first solo project a success only because of Roman's input, not to mention she'd most assuredly end up in his bed.

"Damn you, Roman," she muttered, swiping the sweat from her brow. "You get your wish. I'm outa your house and outa your life."

Yep, as soon as she hobbled back to the house, she'd call around and make arrangements for a place to stay. Decision made.

A big, shiny black truck eased around the corner

behind her. It slowed in the far lane on the narrow road. *Where was her pepper spray when she needed it?*

Most likely back at The Castle, discarded among a multitude of other city-born defenses.

She glanced at the highly polished vehicle with its extended cab and chrome running boards. Not a rusted out junker like the one the teenager drove. Not the kind of truck that ran mud races. The window powered down and the driver leaned out the window, a pair of Ray Ban sunglasses obscuring the intent in his eyes while his broad grin stretched the limits of charm.

"Need a ride, ma'am?"

Ma'am? If he was a pervert, he was a polite one.

"I'm fine, thank you."

"You're limping. I thought you might appreciate a ride."

"I'm fine. Really."

"I'd hate to leave a pretty damsel in distress in the middle of nowhere."

Tess gauged the distance to Roman's driveway as she answered. "I'm no damsel. Nor am I in distress."

"At least you're not arguing with the pretty part."

Her attention snapped to the driver. Clean cut, chiseled cheeks, and no requisite baseball cap covering the wide brow or the healthy crop of dark hair. Just those pricey sunglasses hiding his eyes.

"Save the flattery for someone who's impressed by it, Bubba," she lobbed back at him without slowing her pace.

He laughed a deep, rich laugh. "No one's ever called me 'Bubba'."

"Guess there's a first time for everything."

The truck rolled slowly along in the far lane,

keeping pace with her. She was still several yards from Roman's driveway. Would he hear her if she screamed? Would he come running if he did hear her? Of course he would, even after how she'd treated him. He excelled in damsel rescues.

Maybe she could cut through the woods between the house and road. She eyed the tangled foliage along the roadside.

"That blackberry brush will tear those lovely legs all to hell," her *stalker* said.

She tilted her head toward the stranger in the truck. "Do most of the women you try to pick up run off into the woods?"

Laughter rolled up from deep in his chest. "That's not the usual effect I have on women."

"You can move along, now. I'm fine and really can take care of myself."

"Even an independent woman needs assistance now and then," he drawled.

Didn't she know it?

She shook off the image of Roman's broad shoulders and strong arms and picked up her pace, insisting, "I'm fine."

"I'm sure you are."

"I am."

"I'm just offering a ride."

"I'm not far from home." She lifted her chin toward Roman's driveway, the only one in sight on the stretch ahead. "That's my driveway right there," she said.

"Right there?"

She didn't like the interest with which he noted the driveway and added, "My *husband* is expecting me."

"Husband?"

She gave herself a mental head slap. What was she doing conjuring up an imaginary spouse? She was supposed to be an independent woman capable of defending herself.

A man to lean on.

She winced at the thought. But, since she conjured him up, she might as well make use of the charade.

"Yes. My *husband.* He took advantage of my injured state to beat me back to the house. He so seldom wins our races."

"Competitive. I like that in a woman. Maybe we could run together sometime."

"I'm sure my husband would enjoy that."

The stranger's grin twitched. "If you're okay then—"

"I'm okay."

He gave her a nod, pulled out ahead of her and…turned the big black truck into Roman's driveway.

Tess stopped on the shoulder of the road and uttered an oath. She doubted she'd be lucky enough that the stranger in the black truck would turn around and pull back out of Roman's drive.

By the time she hobbled up to the driver's side of the truck, the stranger had both arms folded over the window frame, his grin crooked.

"You're a friend of Roman's, aren't you?" she demanded.

He nudged the Ray Bans onto the top of his head. "Guilty as charged. Brody McCain."

Mischief twinkled from Brody McCain's blue eyes. She accepted the fingerless leather gloved hand he held out to her and confessed, "And I'm *not* Roman's wife."

"No kidding."

"I'm his…houseguest. Tess Abbot."

He stopped pumping her hand and the laugh lines around his eyes deepened. "Abbot? The architect who hired Roman to renovate The Castle?"

"He told you about me, huh?"

He released her hand, his grin twitching. "Seems he left out a few details."

"Like the fact I don't really have devil's horns?"

"Like the fact you're the gal sharing his house."

He was thinking something else. She saw it in his eyes. Sex. That's what any friend of Roman's to whom he might have gone in the middle of the night for condoms would think.

"You must be a pretty good friend of Roman's," she prompted.

"I like to think of myself as his best friend."

She grimaced. "The kind a guy can turn to in the middle of the night for help…or to borrow something?"

"That's the kind."

"Uh huh."

Brody opened the truck door but didn't jump out. Reaching behind his seat, he lifted out a folded wheelchair. Only then did she notice the additional controls on the steering wheel and the strap holding Brody's legs together.

Tess frowned at the chair popping open as it hit the ground. "I thought you said you *run*."

"Run. Roll. It's all the same to me." He swung himself down into the chair with practiced ease and grinned up at her. "Guess I'm kinda like the *Trojan* horse."

"Trojan, huh?" Tess laughed. "Brody McCain, you are a man full of surprises."

"I was trying for a man of mystery."

"Right." She studied the man who claimed to be Roman's best friend. For an instant something in his eyes hinted there was a lot more to Brody McCain than glib charm. Then it was gone behind a dazzling smile.

He patted the flat black framework of his chair. "What do you think of her?"

"Snazzy rig."

"State of the art design. Titanium frame. Composite wheels." He patted his lap. "Hop aboard. I'll give you a test ride."

"In your dreams," she retorted and limped off toward the house.

"Roman said you had a wicked tongue," he called, rolling after her.

#

Roman watched Tess and Brody from the kitchen window. She'd handled Brody's wheelchair well. Maybe too well. He didn't like the way the two of them laughed together. She never laughed like that with him. Though he'd seen her laugh with her neighbors and occasionally Raymond or another crew member.

He stepped out onto the porch. "You two going to spend the rest of the day out here jabbering?"

"That depends," Brody called from the ramped end of the porch. "Is that fresh baked bread I smell?"

"It is," Roman said.

Brody rolled up the ramp toward Roman, chirping, "I'd have expected you to be in a good mood today, not a bread-baking one."

"Bread-*baking*?" Tess climbed the stairs toward where Roman stood, glancing from him to Brody. "I wouldn't call what he was doing this morning before I left for my run 'baking'. It was more like bread dough *pounding*."

"A man can work off a lot of frustration kneading bread dough," Brody said.

"Watch it," Roman growled. "I can still replace that ramp with steps."

"Do I frustrate you, St. John?" Tess goaded, stopping in front of him, her eyes twinkling with amusement.

"You could frustrate a curse out of monk, Princess?"

"Princess?" Brody asked, approaching them from the side. "Is that official?"

"Only in Roman's mind," she said.

"Ms. Abbot," Roman expanded, "comes from a privileged background. She thinks the world is at her beck and call and us common folk are meant to serve her."

"Another fabrication of his feeble mind," she said and wrinkled her nose at Roman.

"Must be this country air fogging up my head," Roman said. "No, wait, it's smog that chokes out oxygen; smog in the cities."

Brody paused beside Roman and motioned Tess ahead of them through the open door. "Ladies first."

"Stick it in your ear, St. John," Tess lobbed at Roman as she strode past the two men.

Tess disappeared into the house and Roman realized he wasn't the only man on the porch checking out how the bicycle shorts molded to her backside. The hairs on Roman's arms bristled. But before he could say anything about it, Tess trumpeted from inside.

"You baking to feed an army, St. John? There must be half a dozen loaves of bread in here rising or cooling."

Brody grinned up at Roman as he rolled across the threshold. "I'm beginning to understand your baking binge."

Roman stepped in behind his friend, shut the front door, and grabbed the back of Brody's chair, stopping it with a suddenness that almost left skid marks on the linoleum. He'd gone to Brody in the middle of the night for those damn condoms because he was his best friend, his only unmarried friend, and because he had thought Brody could be discreet. He gave Brody a glare that said all that and more.

"You going to make like a good host and feed me?" Brody asked with mock innocence, his eyes on Tess who stood in profile between them and the kitchen table, slim, firm, fetching. "Or just hold me captive inches from heaven?"

"Brodyyyy."

Brody grinned up at him. "Can't wait to sink my teeth into—"

Roman let out a low warning growl.

"—Some of that fresh baked bread," Brody finished.

"It does smell heavenly in here," Tess murmured, nose in the air sniffing.

Roman's growl turned moan-like. She was heaven.

…And hell.

Life was not fair.

She smiled an inscrutable little half smile in his direction. "That's a lot of bread you *kneaded* there, St. John."

"I've got an unwanted houseguest who's frustratingly stubborn and kneading is a great way to burn off my frustration."

"Stubborn?" she returned, planting her hands on her hips.

Brody opened his mouth, but Roman jabbed a silencing finger at his friend. "You just get the butter."

Brody winked and wheeled around the table toward the fridge.

To Tess he said, "I'd ask you to slice one of those loaves of bread, but we don't have all day to argue the point."

"Slicing bread is hardly an issue," she snapped as he strode past her toward the knife block on the countertop beside the stove.

"And I do not argue every point with you," she continued, following him, crowding him.

Roman drew a knife from the block and turned to Tess. She had her hands on her hips and her chin tilting that infuriating challenging angle he'd grown accustomed to. "*This* isn't arguing?"

"*Dammit*, St. John. I can slice bread."

"See what I've had to put up with," Roman said in Brody's direction.

Brody grinned around the refrigerator door at them, waving a shrink wrapped package in the air. "This the only cheese you got?"

"I haven't had a lot of time to stock my cupboards." Roman looked at Tess. "And with an extra mouth to feed these days, supplies don't seem to last as long."

Tess wrinkled her nose at him. "Oh yeah. I eat so much."

He pointed the tip of the serrated knife at her. "You eat plenty for someone who doesn't cook."

"I cook."

He snatched one of the baked loaves of bread off

the counter and snorted. "That's why your garbage was always full of fast food containers."

"You snooped in my garbage?"

"I wrapped it up, as per your orders, then hauled it out to the curb for you."

"I never ordered you to wrap up my garbage. I *asked* you to do it once. As for taking it out to the curb, that was only once a week."

"You hauled out her garbage?" Brody asked with obvious interest, wheeling up to the table with his lap full of condiments, spreads, and cheese.

"I did a lot of things for her that weren't part of the renovating."

Brody grunted. "Don't I know it."

Both Tess and Roman gaped at Brody, and Roman got the distinct impression that Tess had figured out Brody was the guy he'd gotten the condoms from. She was sharp and Brody was playing it unusually obvious today.

Brody dumped his cache of foodstuffs onto the table and nodded at the knife Roman held between him and Tess. "Why don't you let her slice the bread before you wind up doing something that could be construed as assault?"

"Fine," Roman muttered, dumping the loaf of bread and the knife into Tess' hands. "I hope you can handle a knife without hurting yourself."

Tess' right shoulder came up, the one the coat rack had jabbed. "As long as you don't sneak up behind me and startle me, I'll be just fine."

"When did you sneak up on her?" Brody asked.

"I didn't sneak up on her," Roman insisted.

"Yesterday at The Castle," Tess said, cutting him off almost simultaneously.

"All I did was come up to the attic to tell you I

was leaving. Maybe if you weren't someplace you weren't *supposed* to be, you wouldn't have been so jumpy."

She dropped the loaf of bread onto the table. "I had every right to see what damage had been done to my house."

He slapped a cutting board down next to the bread. "The Fire Chief told you to stay out of the attic."

"I was just looking," she countered, driving the knife into the bread, the escaping tendrils of steam reminding Roman how hot she'd been two nights ago and how eager he'd been.

"You disturbed the fire scene," he growled.

"Only because you startled me," she argued, sawing at the bread, "making me trip and fall into that rack so it tipped over on me, skewering me where I couldn't reach!"

An image of her bare flanks and creamy shoulders flashed across the backs of Roman's eyes. Why'd she have to bring up that business that led to her removing her shirt? She slapped a steaming slab of bread into his hand, which all but scalded him.

"See what I've had to put up with all these weeks?" he howled in Brody's direction.

"And you still moved her into your house?"

"*She* moved herself into my house."

Tess threw the knife onto the table and jabbed Roman in the chest with her finger. "You'd said that if you didn't have the remodeling job done on time, I could move into your house."

"Does somebody here need a lawyer?" Brody interjected.

"No," Roman said.

"Maybe," Tess said, at the same time.

"I have some experience arbitrating," Brody supplied.

Tess and Roman both turned on him, but Tess was quicker to speak. "Tell him a verbal agreement is as binding as a written contract."

"You actually told her she could move into your house if the job wasn't done on time?"

"The job would have been done on schedule if not for the fire."

"Which was his fault," she argued.

"Do I smell a lawsuit pending?" Brody quipped.

"Here's your chance, Princess. You, me, and a lawyer all in the same room."

She nodded at Brody. "Is that why you invited him here?"

"I didn't invite him. He showed up on his own."

"Uh huh." She planted her hands on her hips and raised her chin. "Does he do that a lot, show up at opportune times?" She didn't give him time to answer before charging on. "How convenient for you that your best friend is a lawyer. Does he litigate all your lawsuits?"

"I've never had to go to court for a lawsuit."

"Of course not. Your personal lawyer shows up and scares the opposition into settling, right?"

"That's not—"

"Maybe you think this is the way to get me to leave."

"I'm not—"

"Damn right, you're not going to force me out."

She looked so damn smug with her chin thrust out at him, her pupils dilated, and her chest all puffed up. He poked her in the breastbone, the way she always did to him. "If you weren't so damned stubborn, you would have seen how ridiculous your moving in here was in the first place."

"Ridiculous?" Her neck stretched, giving the illusion that she'd grown another inch. "Ridiculous is my being burned out of my house by my contractor."

She jabbed a finger back at him. "Ridiculous is you thinking you're more inconvenienced by this than I am."

He closed his hand around her finger, held it against his chest as he gazed into her eyes. What would she do if he leaned forward right now and kissed those taught lips? Would they go slack? Would their tight line part to admit his tongue? Would she close her eyes, tilt her mouth to the fit of his, and slump against him?

More likely she'd knee him in the groin.

"What's ridiculous is you staying in my house when you can afford the best accommodations any city could offer. In fact, why don't you go back to the city? Given all your complaints about Pine Mountain and its air, you'd be happier."

"You'd like me to disappear, wouldn't you?"

"It's my fondest wish."

She leaned into him, thigh brushing thigh, breast bumping chest. Only the anger sparking from her eyes, the jutting angle of her chin, and click of her teeth gnashing together kept him from enveloping her in his arms and rolling her to the floor beneath him. And Brody's presence. The woman needed to be made love to, and badly.

"Too damned bad," she said, her words squeezing out from between clenched teeth. "Because I'm not going to disappear. I'm not going to leave. I'm going to be a thorn in your side until my house is repaired."

CHAPTER EIGHT

Why had she vowed to stay until her house was fixed when she'd had it all settled in her mind that she was leaving?

Because Roman aggravated her and the oaf didn't deserve a break. Never mind that nagging notion in the back of her mind that there was something else driving her change of mind.

And now, after their lunch of bread and cheese, she was even joining him to inspect a property Brody was considering converting into a sports camp for handicapped kids. She simply couldn't turn down Brody's invitation, especially when smoke had all but spewed from Roman's ears.

But she was having second thoughts now that she was seated between the two men in Brody's truck. The truck hit a bump in the road. Even with its super absorbent shocks, Tess was jostled into Roman.

"Maybe if you belted yourself in, you would stay put," Roman grumbled.

"I am belted in," she fired back at him. "Maybe if your arm wasn't in the way, I wouldn't bump into it."

"It's attached to me. I don't have a lot of options of where to put it."

"I know where I'd like to put it," she muttered, folding her arms across her chest in an effort to create more space between them.

Brody chuckled.

Roman grumbled something about betting he could guess where that would be and placed his arm along the back of the seat. The move reminded her of the night of the fire when Roman had driven her to his house. He'd slung his arm across the back of the seat then, too. Only this time, it was the crook of his arm close to the nape of her neck instead of his fingers. This time, *he* was closer to her.

The truck hit a pothole and Roman's arm bumped her shoulder. Tess' whole body went on alert. She'd had a taste of how thoroughly Roman could touch a woman. He, on the other hand, seemed to be experiencing a different reaction. Judging by the crunch of leather in her ear, Roman had gripped the back of the seat to avoid touching her.

Aggravating him was one thing. Tormenting herself was another. She should have taken her own car, or stayed at his house.

"Do you ski?" Brody asked her as they lumbered down the blacktopped country road.

She nodded, distracted by the lingering yeasty scent of bread that clung to Roman's clothes and the notion all that bread kneading had been because of her.

"The property we'll be looking at is adjacent to the local ski hill," Brody went on. "That way we can use the resort facilities for our downhill ski program."

"Sounds like you've thought this out pretty well," she said, distracted by that strong, hairy arm behind her head that had cradled her from the hard floor at the foot of her bed and held her when she'd confessed her greatest fears.

"I may even have Roman talked into being my ski instructor."

Tess gave Roman a sidelong look. "I didn't know you skied."

"There's a lot about me you don't know."

That was true. She knew little about Roman other than that he was a reliable and excellent contractor, a diehard family man with a bunch of siblings, a pretty good cook who baked great bread, a nice guy, and hot.

"He's a world class ski instructor," Brody supplied.

"World class? Really?" she questioned, openly studying Roman.

Roman stared out the front windshield, muttering, "She doesn't want to know about my past."

"What's the matter, St. John, got something to hide?" she goaded.

He regarded her through narrowed eyes. "My past is an open book. How about yours, Princess? I've never heard you talk about your life in the big city, though you've said plenty about how Pine Mountain lacks in comparison to Chicago."

"Maybe if you'd ever lived in a city, you'd understand my frustration with repair services that don't work nights or weekends, taxicab companies that have only one vehicle, and mosquitoes that suck the lifeblood out of a person."

"As opposed to high-priced repair services, parking shortages that make a person dependent on taxis, and roaches big enough to carry off your first born?" Roman countered.

"You have no Chinese takeout, no sushi bars, no Starbucks—"

"No winos, muggers, or graffiti, either," Roman leveled back at her.

"You have no night life," she retorted. "No all-night restaurants. No singles bars. No live entertainment."

"Sometimes—"

"The city hums with life," she said, cutting him off.

"Small towns are safe and quiet," he grumbled.

"Oh, yes. All that quiet you can't shut off."

"Many people like quiet, Princess," he muttered.

She rolled her eyes. "There's only one thing worse than the silence. That blasted bird that sings me awake before dawn every morning."

"That's a whippoorwill." Roman said.

"I don't care if it's the goose that lays the golden egg. If I get my hands on it, I'm going to wring its scrawny neck."

"And there's the local ski hill," Brody interjected, as though she and Roman weren't about to wring each other's necks.

"And those are the condos I told you about," Roman said, pointing at a cluster of buildings at the base of the forested hill striped with wide vertical clearings. "Probably no whippoorwills around here."

"Is that a hint?" she asked.

"Looks like the parking area is well lit," he said.

"I'm not moving out," she said.

"And that towering structure visible above the tree line ahead," Brody supplied like some single-minded tour guide, "is our world famous ski jump."

"Just to aggravate me, you'd rather suffer whippoorwills and mosquitoes," Roman countered, ignoring Brody's travelogue.

And a contractor who wears happy face pajama bottoms. Just the memory of what she'd found beneath those happy faces made her stomach pinch with desire. What was wrong with her, wanting a man who insulted her at every turn?

What was wrong with her that she stayed just to spite him?

"Dammit, St. John," she snapped in frustration. "The fire was your responsibility. I'm staying."

"I've never known a woman as stubborn as you." Roman said.

"That ski jump," Brody went on as though she and Roman weren't waging their own personal war, "hosts an annual world class event right here in little old Pine Mountain."

"You just don't like that I'm holding you to your word," she huffed out at Roman.

"I used to ski jump," Brody continued. "So did Roman."

In unison, Roman and Tess looked at Brody.

"That's how Roman and I met." Brody said.

Tess looked up at the scaffold-like structure looming into view at the top of a very steep hill. "Roman used to jump off that?"

Roman let out a low, warning growl. Clearly, Brody wasn't listening to him as he continued with, "Once or twice. Though Pine Mountain wasn't exactly our old stomping grounds."

The last thing Roman needed was for Brody to give Tess more ammunition to use against him. "She doesn't want to hear about my ski jumping days, Brody."

"The hell I don't," she said. "This is an entirely unexpected side of you."

"It's not a side of me. It was just something I tried when I was young and foolish."

"Foolish, huh?" She studied him with a smugness he didn't like. Then she turned to Brody. "Continue."

Brody grinned over Tess' head at him. He didn't like Brody's smugness, either.

"I'd just finished a jump by skidding face first down a hill almost as big as the one we have here."

"Ouch," Tess intoned.

Roman groaned and turned his face to the side window.

"I rode the gondola back to the top with Roman. The whole way, he tried to talk me out of taking my second jump. You'd have thought he was my father, the way he carried on."

Sarcasm dripped from Tess', "Roman patronizing. Who'd a thunk it?"

"You were dazed," Roman muttered. "You should have pulled out for the rest of the day. You could have had a concussion."

"I thought he was trying to get me to quit because I was his toughest competition." Brody snorted. "He just wanted to keep me from scrambling my brains."

"Are you sure that was his motive?" Tess asked.

"Always quick to doubt me, huh, Princess?" Roman countered.

Brody accelerated around a long sweeping curve, the centrifugal force pressing Tess into Roman's side. Every muscle in Roman's body tightened against the assault of her body on his, and he glared at Brody.

Brody went on as though Roman and Tess hadn't been on the verge of starting World War III and he'd just maneuvered them into no-man's land. "I was a hotshot nineteen year old riding the testosterone bullet. I was sure I could win that competition because I wasn't afraid to ride the hill out."

"You mean you were foolish enough to think you could ride the hill to the bottom," Roman argued, trying to shame Brody into silence.

"You see, if you ride the hill too far," Brody explained for Tess' benefit, "if you land where the angle of the hill begins to break, the impact is harder. A skier's injury risk rises dramatically."

"And Roman didn't want you to out ski him, right?"

Roman cursed under his breath.

"Not exactly," Brody said.

"Leave it be, Brody," Roman muttered.

"When he saw that he couldn't talk me out of riding the hill beyond its limit, he gave me some advice about how to handle landing close to the break."

"And?"

"I followed his advice. I didn't fall even though I out-rode the hill."

"So you won the tournament?"

Brody turned off the main road, chuckling. "No, I didn't win. Roman took first place."

"But you out-rode the hill," she said.

"So did Roman."

She huffed. "Didn't I say he wanted you out of the competition?"

"I wasn't trying to eliminate him from the competition. I just didn't want him to break his fool neck," Roman said.

"But *you* pushed the limit of the hill."

Roman slumped against the door. "I caught a tail wind. I rode it further than I should have."

He met Tess' steady gaze. She seemed to be measuring him. Oddly, he didn't want to be found lacking. "I had myself a few wild and rowdy days. So shoot me."

The truck jerked to a halt in front of a squat, two-story house with peeling paint and wide wrap around porches.

"This is it," Brody announced. "North Point. A camp where handicapped kids can come and be with other kids like them." Brody grinned at Roman and

Tess. "Providing the two of you agree she's sound enough to renovate."

"Agree? Us?" Roman wrenched open the passenger side door and jumped out. "You've got to be kidding."

Brody leaned over the steering wheel and grinned at Roman. "And here I thought you two would make a great team. A carpenter and an architect."

Roman slapped the truck door and headed toward the house, trying to outdistance Tess' and Brody's voices but failing miserably.

"What is *his* problem?" Tess demanded.

Brody's grin twitched. "Not enough bread."
#
Roman was at the door before he realized he didn't have the key. He cursed. He cursed Tess for accepting Brody's invitation. He cursed Brody for his big mouth. But most of all, he cursed himself for agreeing to work with her in the first place when he still found Tess Abbot so distracting.

Muscles low in his groin tightened. His fingers flexed around the flashlight he'd brought from home and he glowered back at the truck where Tess lingered in the cab with Brody—Brody with his damnable smirk and big mouth. He was probably filling her in on some of their rowdy exploits of those early years. Or maybe he was telling her about how they reconnected years later when Brody needed his house made wheelchair friendly. He didn't need Tess Abbot hearing Brody's Saint Roman speech, either.

"Are you two coming or not?" he yelled.

Tess slid across the seat and out of the truck. Brody leaned through his window and called back, "You two will understand if I wait for you here."

Him and Tess, alone again. What had he done to

deserve this kind of aggravation?

She stopped in front of him and dangled the house key in his face.

"Be my guest," he said, stepping aside.

She moved to the door and bent to fit the key to the lock. She still wore her running shirt knotted up around her waist. But the back of the shirt rode up from the waistband of the jeans she'd changed into— the cheap jeans she'd bought at The Bargain Mart. Correction, the jeans *he'd* bought for her. They rode low on her back as she bent, rode low and buckled away from her skin.

He had no business following the path of her spine into that space below their waistband. But something just above the edge of her panty line caught his eye. A tramp stamp? It was a tattoo of a rose. Damned if he didn't want to ease the jeans down her hips and trace each bright red petal with a fingertip.

"Unusually wide for how old it is," she said, straightening.

"What?" he asked, blinking.

She indicated the door she'd swung open. "The door. It's wider than was normally used in a house of this age."

"Good," he muttered. "That's one less we have to widen to meet code."

"And to accommodate wheelchairs." She turned and scanned the wraparound porch. "The place could be ramped easily without losing the aesthetic appeal of the original design."

"You weren't all that interested in aesthetics when you were renovating The Castle." He edged past her into the house. She followed.

"The hell I wasn't."

"You knocked a wall out between two bedrooms to make a master suite and turned the nursery into a walk-in closet," he argued, testing the floorboards beneath his feet for spongy spots.

"That had nothing to do with aesthetics. That was about making an old house more attractive to today's home buyer," Tess countered, her gaze traveling along the seams where the walls and ceiling met, no doubt checking for corners out of square.

"You could have maintained the integrity of the house and still sold it," he said, stroking the wide woodwork framing the archway between front room and dining area, appreciating its solidness.

"Maybe I didn't have time to wait around for the kind of buyer who'd appreciate small, cozy rooms." She stepped into the dining room and faced him. "Besides, it wasn't your house and, therefore, not your choice to make."

She stood there in front of him, hands on her hips and chin defiantly cocked. He could point out that the privilege of money afforded people a lot more choices. But something in her eyes didn't match her pose. Something in their deep brown depths hinted of panic. Maybe she wasn't as solvent as he'd thought.

"You're right," he said. "It isn't my house."

He moved past her into the kitchen. When she followed him, he asked, "Don't you have something to inspect?"

"I can do my walk through with you."

"Swell."

He opened the cabinet under the sink and inspected the plumbing. It took him longer than it should have because his attention kept wandering around the kitchen with the sound of Tess' footsteps.

"So you were a ski jumper," she said from across

the room.

"I was a ski instructor who did some ski jumping for the thrill of it when I was young and dumb." He rolled onto his back in the confining space under the sink and shined his flashlight at the joints where sink and plumbing met.

"And where did you do all that?" she asked from another location in the kitchen.

"At a ski hill."

"No kidding."

He heard a cupboard door slam shut.

"Was it in Colorado?" Thump went another cupboard door.

"No."

"Lake Placid? Sun Valley? Banff?" Thump. Thump. Thump.

"No, no, and no."

"Can we at least narrow it down to the North American continent?"

Her voice was getting closer. He glanced down the length of his legs and spied hers beside his. Stubborn and persistent. The woman was not going to stop.

"Europe," he said. "I was a ski instructor at a number of European resorts."

"Europe, huh? There're some big hills over there. I'm impressed."

"Big hills. Big resorts. You got it."

"You must have been a good skier."

"Very good."

"How'd you wind up working abroad?"

He slid out from under the sink, searching her face for sarcasm. All he found was genuine curiosity.

"My parents were in the diplomatic corps," he said and climbed to his feet.

"Diplomatic corps." She whistled.

"Don't get too impressed." He opened the back door and tested the porch boards. "They were support staff."

"Must have been an interesting life."

He smiled to himself. "Yeah. It was interesting."

"But you quit ski jumping," she prodded. "Why?"

His expression turned serious. "It was the safe thing to do. The responsible thing. We should check out the attic."

In the largest of the upstairs rooms, Roman nudged aside the small trap door in the ceiling of the closet. He stared into the darkness beyond the opening. "You didn't happen to notice a ladder or stool during our tour of the house, did you?"

Tess edged into the closet beside him, letting the ratty drape that served as a door fall into place behind her. "Not so much as a chair."

"You're never going to boost me up through that," he said.

"Guess that means I'm elected," she said. "Thread those fingers together and give me a lift, St. John."

He gave her a glum look.

"You don't doubt that I can inspect that attic as well as you, do you?"

"No, Princess. I'm sure you're every bit as capable as I am at spotting dry rot and stress problems." *I just don't relish getting close enough to you to hoist you into the attic.*

Threading his fingers together, he squatted and offered Tess a foothold. She placed her foot in his hands. Though she wore tennis shoes, he could remember what her bare arch had felt like against his palm.

She placed her hands on his shoulders, reminding

him of the soft touch of her fingers when she had been exploring him. If he lifted his head right now, he could bury his face between her breasts.

"Your back seize up on you or something, St. John?"

"Just waiting for you to give me the go ahead," he grumbled.

"Fine. I'm re—"

He rose, launching her upward. She shrieked.

As her head disappeared into the attic, he called up to her, "I hope you're not squeamish about bats."

Sitting on the lip of the opening, she peered down at him. "You'd like it if I was, wouldn't you?"

"A guy can dream."

"Just give me the flashlight, St. John."

He handed the light up to her. She pulled her legs up into the attic.

"And watch where you step," he shouted up at her. "I've got enough to do with this place without having to patch ceilings."

"Get lost," she yelled back.

"Remember, I'm the only one here who can help you down from there."

Silence answered. He waited a minute, then, "What's it look like up there?"

"Dark."

"Funny. What else?"

"So far no water stains. No rot."

A little while later he called again, "Find anything, yet?"

"Not so much as a bat dropping," she called from the depths of the attic. "Hope you're not too disappointed."

The minutes stretched. He tried to make himself wait. But she could be in trouble up there. "You still alive up there?"

Her head appeared in the opening. "If you don't stop interrupting me, St. John, I'm never going to get this inspection done."

"Excuse me, Your Highness, for being concerned about your well-being."

"Isn't there something else you can occupy yourself with?"

"Fine. Don't blame me if there's no one here to help you down when you're ready."

Roman gave the second floor a quick inspection. When he returned to the master bedroom, Tess' legs were dangling from the attic opening. He moved into the closet and slid his hands up her thighs. She screamed and came plummeting down on top of him, the flashlight smacking him in the head. He stumbled backwards out of the closet, taking the curtained door, curtain rod, and Tess to the floor with him. Of course Tess was on top of him.

She squirmed, her backside in perfect alignment with his crotch. "Ow," he protested. "You didn't have to panic. I had you."

"I didn't panic. I had everything under control until you grabbed me and startled me."

"So this is my fault, too?"

She struggled to dislodge them from curtain and rod. He pushed at her derriere.

"Quit manhandling me," she grumbled. "I can get up on my own."

"Then do it."

#

Roman strode up to Brody's open window. "You had to come and check her out, didn't you?"

"You pledged abstinence until Miss Right came along. Then you beat my door down in the middle of the night looking for condoms. You bet I wanted to see the woman you've chosen to spend the rest of your life with."

"It's not her."

"Could have fooled me."

"She's a royal pain in the ass."

"A royal knockout you want bad, you mean." Brody glanced up at the house. "So, where is the royal pain?"

"Inspecting the crawl space under the house."

"By herself?"

"I only had the one flashlight and, get this; she said she wouldn't trust the job to a contractor, that she needed to inspect the foundation for herself. I also had to trust her to check out the attic for me."

"Let me get this straight. She's crawling around the dirt under the house while you're standing out here?"

"I offered."

"And you sent *her* into the attic to do that dirty work as well."

"There was no ladder and she sure as hell couldn't hoist me up."

Brody snorted. "What the hell happened the other night?"

Roman slumped against the fender of the truck. "Nothing."

Brody laughed.

"It isn't funny," Roman said. "She changed her mind."

"And you didn't."

"I would have if I'd been thinking straight. Bad idea, her and me."

"So, you're mad because she figured that out first?"

"I'm mad because I'm a damned sucker. I let her move in because I felt responsible. I invited her back because I felt sorry for her. Heck, I even cleaned out her fridge for her. And all she does is complain. She's driving me crazy."

"So, seduce her again."

An image of him and Tess naked on his guestroom floor slammed through Roman. He frowned at the ground. "I wasn't the one doing the seducing."

"Aaah. She tested your abstain-until-Miss-Right comes along, and you failed. That's what you're mad about."

"I'm not mad," Roman insisted.

"That's right. You're frustrated. All that bread." Brody laughed.

"I'm glad you're having fun at my expense," Roman grumbled.

"If you're frustrated, do a little trolling in the local bars. You'll have no trouble picking up something to relieve that pressure built up in your pants."

"Oh, yeah. And when I bring my pressure reliever home for the night, how do you propose I explain Her Royal Pain?"

"I could take her off your hands for a night. I'm not without my charms."

Roman scowled at Brody. "You've done enough."

Brody laughed again.

"What's so funny?"

"You are, man. You're jealous."

"Go to hell."

"You want her so bad, you can't see straight."

"I'll show you how straight I can see. Have at her.

Seduce her."

"Won't work."

"Why not?"

"Because, in spite of my charms, the gal has eyes only for you. Somewhere in that thick skull of yours, you know it, or you wouldn't have offered me a shot at her."

"You don't know what you're talking about."

"When we were talking about ski jumping, she didn't once ask me how I managed that while in a wheelchair."

"You weren't in the chair back then."

"Yeah. You know that and I know that. But the lady was focused so much on you, she didn't even ask about me. When I tried to pick her up on the road, she even said she was married to you."

"What?!"

"Yeah, I think she said it because she thought I was some sort of creep following her when she was running."

Tess Abbot, the houseguest from hell, the woman who'd sworn to be a thorn in his side, interested in him? No way.

Yet, Roman couldn't help but wonder. After all, she had made the first move the night of the storm. *She'd* asked *him* to stay.

He glanced up at the house and thought about her in the dark crawl space by herself. Sometimes he could be a jerk.

"I'd better go check on her."

#

Once more, Tess wrenched against whatever had snagged the back of her jeans. Once more, she failed to break free.

She thumped her forehead against the packed dirt

of the crawl space, muttering, "Hell. Hell. Hell."

That's exactly where she was…in contractor hell. Specifically she was in Roman St. John's contractor hell. And he was the only one around who could help her.

"Hell. Hell. Hell."

If only she could reach…

She tried to angle her arm back to where she was snagged. Once again, her elbow connected with the low floor joist. She couldn't let Roman find her like this. She'd never hear the end of it.

"Is that your little derriere wedged in there, Princess?"

She groaned. "I'm not wedged in here."

"Looks pretty tight to me, the space that is."

She swung the flashlight back at Roman. He was standing where the crawl space under the house had been dug out to make a small basement, grinning.

"Something hooked me," she said.

"And here I didn't even know it was princess season."

"If that's some sort of reference to fishing, St. John, go jump in a lake."

"I don't think you really want me to do that, Princess, at least not until I've gotten you out of your predicament. Shine your flashlight on whatever snagged you."

She fumbled with the flashlight.

"Not in my eyes," Roman groused. "Shine it on your backside."

"You getting a thrill out of this, St. John?"

"I'm enjoying it, if that's what you mean."

"Try crawling in here and enjoying *it* a little closer," she said.

"If I get wedged in there with you, we're both

going to be in big trouble."

"I told you, I'm not wedged in here. I'm hung up on something."

"Try wriggling around a little," he said.

"Gee, why didn't I think of that?"

"Didn't work, huh?"

"Just get in here and tell me what I'm hung up on."

She heard him shimmy in beside her. "Hand me that flashlight...carefully. My skull has had enough of a pounding today."

She opened her mouth to tell him what he could do with the flashlight, but decided she wasn't in any position to tell him to shove it.

"This is a heck of a fix you got yourself in," he said, the flashlight beam bobbing against the joists above her and his hand sliding across her backside.

"That hand on my ass had better be necessary, St. John."

"Maybe you'd prefer I hook you up to a come-along and winch you out of there."

"Just get me out of here."

He pressed down on her backside. "Looks like a big splinter snagged your belt loop."

"Just tell me which way I need to crawl to get unhooked."

"You mean you'd follow my orders? That'd be a first."

Was that laughter she heard in his voice? Damn the man.

"Just tell me, do I crawl forward or shimmy backward?" she asked.

"I vote for you shimmying backward."

"You're having way too much fun with this."

His fingers splayed across the space just below

the waistband of her jeans, leaving hot little trails across her skin. "I don't know how you did it, but your belt loop is twisted around the splinter. I'm going to have to cut the loop."

"These jeans aren't even a week old."

"You know, Princess, if I didn't know better, I'd almost think you're on a budget."

If he only knew how close to the truth that was.

"Just cut through the splinter."

He sawed at the splinter with his pocketknife, his forearms, wrists, and the heels of his hands rubbing back and forth across her buttocks. She was in heaven.

She was in hell.

Finally, the splinter gave.

"There you go, Princess."

Given the swing of the flashlight beam and the receding scuffing sounds, she could tell he was shimmying out. She shimmied backward a few inches only to find her shirt was riding up on her. She started forward.

"I wouldn't go that way if I were you, Princess. What's left of that backside grabbing splinter might snatch you up again."

"I realize you'd prefer I go out backward, but I crawl forward better."

"You go forward and you're going to get hung up again."

"I can be careful—"

His hands closed on her ankles.

"Let go of me."

"This is for your own good, Princess. Put your head down."

He tugged. She shrieked. He pulled. Her shirt rode up around armpits and dirt collected in her sports bra.

When he had her clear of the crawl space, she swatted him away and tugged the shirt down into place as he laughed.

So much for aggravating Roman St. John.

CHAPTER NINE

The alarm clock on the nightstand next to Roman's head chirped. Face buried in his pillow, he slapped the annoying object silent and cursed his inability to ignore Tess.

She'd filled his dreams with sensations of her hands caressing him, soft and cool as silk, and her mouth on his, hungry and hot. She'd plagued his waking hours with images of her little derriere trapped in the crawl space of Brody's prospective camp...and of her t-shirt pushed up to her armpits.

He groaned and hammered the pillow to either side of his head. It shouldn't have mattered to him that she'd accepted Brody's invitation to talk about his project over dinner. He shouldn't have waited up last night for Tess to get home from Brody's. What hours she kept weren't his business.

Yet, he had waited up until he heard her car pull into the driveway. Then he'd feigned sleep as she crept past his door and up the steps to the guest bedroom.

Much as he hated to admit it, Brody was right. He was jealous. He wanted her laughing and dining with him, not his friend.

He wanted her in his bed where he could explore the rose tattoo on her tailbone and the ring in her belly button.

He wanted to bury himself so deep inside her it would take a month of Sundays to dig himself out of her. All night, he'd struggled with that need. That's what he got for sampling her firm curves and silky skin. An insatiable desire for a prickly tongued goddess.

In spite of how miserable she made him, he throbbed beneath the happy face pajama bottoms. Physical need. Nagging...teasing...tormenting.

He groaned and vaulted out of bed.

He needed a cold shower.

He dug into his underwear drawer for a fresh pair of shorts. Oddly, the pair of jockey shorts he took off the top of the pile appeared brighter than the next pair. Maybe it was the dim light of false dawn that made that second pair in the stack appear dull by comparison.

He held the bright set next to the dull pair in the drawer. Same shadows. Same dim light. Yet the pair in his hand was stark white next to the pair still folded in the drawer. That was odd...

Then he remembered Tess saying she'd washed his shorts.

#

The bedroom door slammed open against the wall, jolting Tess awake. By the time her eyes focused, Roman was standing at the side of her bed shaking something that looked suspiciously like jockey shorts over her.

"Why are my shorts pink?"

"Shorts?" she mumbled, her focus fixing on his chest...his very bare chest.

"Yeah," he snapped. "My shorts. They're pink. Why?"

Tess stared at Roman's naked stomach. She had a vague sense of dreaming about those hard abs. Or had the dream been about another equally hard part of Roman's anatomy? Now that was an *aggravation* she wouldn't mind.

She glanced past the fist gripping the pink shorts and down his washboard firm abdominal wall. The deep dimple of his belly button peeked at her from above the low riding happy face pajama bottoms. Oh yeah. She'd like to tug those pjs down off his hips and see if she was still dreaming.

The shorts filled her field of vision again and Roman shouted, "What happened to my shorts?"

So much for the illusion of dreams.

She pushed herself up onto her elbows and grumbled, "You burst into my room without knocking over a pair of shorts?"

"*Pink* shorts!"

"What if I'd been dressing?"

He bent low over her, putting his face close to hers. "It's before dawn. The whippoorwill isn't even up yet. I took a chance you'd still be in bed."

She wrinkled her nose at him. "So you woke me up on purpose? Gee, thanks. So, what's your problem?"

"Pink shorts," he said, shoving the offending underwear in her face.

Tess slumped back against her pillow. "You finally worked your way down to the shorts I washed, huh?"

The pair of shorts in Roman's fist shuddered. "What did you wash them in?"

She yawned and drew the sheet up under her chin. "More like what I washed them with."

"And that would be?" he demanded with annoying persistence.

"Your burgundy towels."

"Why on earth would you wash white shorts with burgundy towels?"

There was that damnable laundry issue again. Tess scowled and let her eyes drift shut.

"Only a moron would wash whites and colors together," he said.

Her eyelids flew open. First the man calls her a Princess, then a shrew, and now a moron. Not even her father had ever called her stupid. He'd refused to acknowledge her talents, but he had at least found her award-winning design of merit...as long as said design had been presented by her fiancé. Make that former fiancé. Men!

"I washed them," Tess said into the face hovering inches above her. "They're clean. You could at least be grateful for that."

"But they're *pink*. I am not going to wear pink underwear."

"Fine then. Don't wear them." She closed her eyes with finality.

"All I have left in my underwear drawer are pink shorts," he protested, flapping the offending shorts. The breeze they caused was annoying.

She rolled over, putting her back to him, "Then buy new ones."

"*You* ruin my clothes," he growled in her ear, making it itch, "and expect *me* to buy my own replacements?"

"I expect you to leave me alone," she muttered and tugged the sheet over her head. He tore it back from her.

"I am not going to buy new shorts." His growl against the back of her ear sent a delicious shiver down her spine. "*You* are going to buy me new shorts."

She rolled toward him and sat up with such speed she almost knocked heads with him. "But—"

"You caused the problem," he said, jerking back from her. "You fix it." He tossed the shorts in her lap, imparting over his shoulder as he headed for the door, "You'll find the size on the waistband." He paused in the doorway, a study in bronze as the dawn broke through her window and washed over him. "And, Princess, this time use your own credit card."

#

Any man who woke her before sunrise and ordered her to buy him new underwear had to pay. Trouble was, Tess hadn't yet figured out the optimum retaliation for Roman. But the Franklin and Son Men's Emporium held promise.

Tess stood in the narrow, slanting center aisle of the aged store giving the yellowed, fourteen-foot ceilings, wall lined shelves, and racks of dark suits to either side of the aisle a once over. Maybe she'd thought any underwear from Pine Mountain's mecca of men's wear would be made of plaid flannel or, better yet, wool. Oh the justice of Roman scratching himself raw.

But Franklin and Son Men's Emporium didn't harbor a single piece of plaid. Maybe she should have gone to The Bargain Mart. Cheap underwear might have done the trick. Cheap. Skimpy. Binding.

She was about to turn around and walk out when a slight built man who appeared to be as old as the building stepped out from behind one of the suit racks. "May I help you?"

She gave his perfectly tailored suit a once over only to discover he was doing the same to her. When he finished, he raised one eyebrow at her. Obviously, her Bargain Mart jeans and blouse didn't measure up to his standards.

"I need shorts," she replied.

The shopkeeper smiled solicitously. "We sell only men's clothing here, my dear."

"That's what I want. Jockey shorts. Men's."

The old man flushed and screwed his mouth up so tight his lips seemed to disappear. Hadn't this guy ever helped a woman buy her husband underwear before?

Behind the aged clerk appeared a younger version of the pinched face. Only the thin lips on this face smiled. "Pop, Mr. Henson's in back waiting for his fitting. I'll take care of the lady."

The son of Franklin and Son Men's Emporium, no doubt.

Young Franklin ushered her toward a glassed in case at the back of the store. Discreetly shelved behind the display cases in neat stacks was the men's underwear. No wonder the elder Franklin just about swallowed his face when she asked about men's jockey shorts.

"What size do you require, Miss?"

"Thirty-fours."

"Jockey style you said, correct?"

"Yes." At least junior didn't suffer the same queasiness about talking underwear with a woman as did the senior Franklin.

Young Franklin handed her a packaged threesome that were definitely superior to the brand she'd turned pink. But that wasn't the reason she'd ventured into the Men's Emporium. She just hadn't put her finger on what she'd thought she'd find in a small town store that specialized in men's wear.

"Perhaps madam would like colored."

She smiled at junior. "Perhaps I would."

Junior set another package on the counter next to the white ones. "We stock navy as well."

Tess' smile faded. Much as buying Roman colored shorts would serve him right for waking her out of a dead sleep before dawn to complain about pink shorts, navy just didn't seem a strong enough statement.

As though reading her mind, Junior supplied, "If you don't mind a less familiar brand, we do stock a more...adventurous selection."

"Adventurous?"

She must have revealed her interest in the inflection of her voice as Junior's thin lips curled conspiratorially at their outer corners. "I think I have just what you want down here."

He nodded for her to follow him to the far end of the glassed display case where he retrieved a plastic box from the base of the display case.

"I keep these in stock for *special* clients." Junior lifted the lid off the box.

Tess stared at the assortment of men's underwear in the box. Leopard print briefs, slick skimpy silks, and...There to one side, little more than a black string...Tess grinned and plucked the thong underwear from the box and dangled it in the air to her own and Junior's delight.

"I think these will do nicely."

#

Roman stepped out of the shower and toweled off. At least the hot water had eased some of the day's tension from his shoulders, tension that had started first thing this morning with the discovery of his pink shorts.

Then the lumberyard had shorted his order. Banking during his lunch hour, he discovered the deposit check on the current job had bounced. It'd taken two hours to track down the client and straighten out the finances. Delays he didn't need when he was already short-handed due to Cousin Raymond's light duty status until his thumb was fully healed.

Roman knotted the towel around his waist and headed across the hall to his room. To cap his day off, he'd met Tess at The Castle only to be stood up by the Fire Marshal. Her Royal Pain in the Butt had screeched like a howler monkey all the while he was on his cell phone tracking down the Fire Marshal who, it turned out, had ended up in the emergency room being treated for an allergic reaction to a bee sting. What more could go wrong?

He eyed his underwear drawer. *Let there be clean, white shorts in there for tomorrow.*

He opened the drawer. It was empty.

"God help you, Tess Abbot, if you haven't bought me any shorts."

Roman charged up the steps and hit the upstairs bedroom door with a fist. The door flew open, catching Tess in the middle of shimmying into a close-fitting camisole.

In the instant it took Roman to register her state of undress, in the instant before he turned his back on her, her image burned into his mind. The sweetly tapered back his hands had stroked four nights ago. The gentle curve of the spine his fingers had mapped. The blood red rose at the base of that spine peeking at him from the lacey edge of a mere scrap of pale yellow panty.

Roman tried to force the image of Tess Abbot's nearly naked body from his head...and his tingling fingertips...and the male member twitching beneath his bath towel.

"Twice in one day, St. John? Is this going to be a

habit with you?"

"Sorry," he muttered over his shoulder. "I knocked."

"Once."

"The door swung open before I could knock a second time," he said.

"This being your house, I'd have thought you'd be aware of all its little idiosyncrasies, like an ill-fitting catch."

"I said I was sorry," he growled, turning and advancing on her, too late remembering the state of undress she'd been in when he'd burst into the room. At least she'd put on a robe, the short, slinky one that barely covered her and that scrap of yellow panty.

He forced himself to think about the business at hand, his shorts...or rather the lack of them and demanded, "Where are my shorts?"

"You said you would not wear pink shorts. I got rid of them."

"I also asked you to buy me new shorts today."

"You didn't ask, you ordered."

"Ordered. Asked. Whatever. Just tell me you bought me new underwear."

"I bought you new underwear, St. John."

"Where are they?"

"Right here," she purred, lifting an ominously small bag from the clutter of female products on top of the dresser.

He read the black lettering on the green paper bag. "You bought me underwear from the Men's Emporium?"

He snatched the bag from her fingers. "There are cheaper places to shop."

"But Franklin and Son Men's Emporium has the finest quality."

Roman frowned at the bag that barely filled his palm. "What'd you do, buy me just one pair of shorts?"

"Of course not. I bought you six."

He dug in the bag, his frown deepening as he pulled out one of the thongs. "What the hell is this?"

"A thong," she chimed. "It's the latest thing in undergarments for men as well as for women." She pulled another thong from the bag and stretched out the narrow cord that comprised the back of the garment. "See. It leaves no panty line."

"Do I look like a man concerned with panty lines?"

She glanced down at the towel barely covering his modesty. He resisted the urge to fold his hands over the place where the family jewels twitched in protest. His heart and mind may be willing to abstain, but that conscienceless part of his anatomy didn't like being out of commission.

"Okay. You've had your fun," he muttered. "Now where are the real shorts?"

"These are as real as you're going to get."

"You can't be serious."

"You commanded me to buy you shorts. I bought you shorts."

He dangled the thong in her face. "These do not qualify as jockey shorts."

"The man at Franklin's considered them shorts."

"Junior no doubt. He's into alternatives. Just ask his significant other, Vincent. I'm not."

"Variety is the spice of life."

"I'll spice up my life in my own way, thank you very much."

"Ah yes. Ski jumper and world class ski instructor. Had yourself quite a run in your oat sowing days, didn't you? Got it all out of your system?"

"All out of my system. You got it."

"Put all your little boy toys away, huh?"

"It's the sort of thing grown-ups do."

"And what is your grown up idea of spicing up life? Taking out the garbage on Tuesday instead of Friday? Or maybe it's the day you rotate your mattress?"

Mattress. Bed. That's where he wanted to be. In his bed. Him and Tess between the sheets. How was that for grown up thoughts?

More like his thoughts had just taken a bad turn into Never-Never-Land.

"Look," he prodded more gently, "I don't suppose I could talk you into washing out the few white shorts I have."

"How about you wash your own shorts?" she simpered back at him.

"It's late. I need to get some sleep. I have to be on the site tomorrow by five a.m. What if I throw them in the washer and you toss them into the dryer when they're done?"

She yawned. "I'd like to help you out, St. John. But somebody woke me up this morning at the crack of dawn. I just can't seem to keep my eyes open."

"Just tell me where the pink shorts are."

"In the garbage."

"Fine." He turned for the steps.

"Not your garbage."

He regarded her narrowly. "What do you mean, *not my garbage*?"

"Given your hyper-sensitivity to the color pink, I thought it prudent that I didn't put them in your garbage. Wouldn't want anyone getting the wrong idea about you, now would we?"

"Where are they?"

"I put them in my garbage."

"At The Castle?"

"That's where my garbage is and I do have a lot of garbage these days, thanks to you."

Roman groaned. "What the hell am I supposed to wear for underwear tomorrow?"

Tess dangled the thong in front of his face.

"That is not going to fit me."

She slid her hand into the front pocket of the thong, flexing her fingers until she stretched the silky sack to capacity. "Feels like the perfect fit to me."

And she would know. She'd *handled* him to a fever pitch only a few nights ago on the very spot where he now stood. He tensed just thinking about the silky exploration of her fingers around his...

He snatched the thong from her fingers and wheeled for the steps.

"Sweet dreams," she called after him.

The bag full of thongs crushed in his fist.

CHAPTER TEN

"You're walking kinda funny there, Roman," Cousin Raymond said. "Did the black widow finally castrate you?"

He walked away without comment. That was the sort of thing Roman had contended with all day. Though none of the guys had guessed the real reason he walked funny was because he wore thong underwear that felt like more like a rope between his butt cheeks. But they all knew about Tess staying at his house, thanks to Brody telling Raymond.

Roman climbed into his truck. It would be a cold day in hell before he trusted Brody with any more of his secrets.

He started the truck and turned it in the direction of The Bargain Mart. He'd buy his own damn underwear, Tess Abbot and her thongs be damned.

Though, by afternoon, he had begun to get used to the coarse scrape of denim against his backside and the slick slip and slide of the thong pocket cradling his most personal assets. At the oddest moments, he'd recall the way his houseguest had nestled her fingers into the sack of the thong, fingers she'd once closed around his arousal.

The memory made him jerk within the slick pouch—made him recall how she'd stood over him naked, wet, and ready. He wanted to chase the harpy away and make Tess Abbot abandon herself to that passionate woman who'd been intent on taking him on the floor of his guestroom. What would she do if he walked into the house, caught her up in his arms, and kissed her?

She'd probably smack him into next week.

He grimaced. He didn't need any more blows to his ego. She'd battered that enough in the weeks since they met to last him a lifetime.

The lit sign for The Bargain Mart loomed to his right. He slammed on his brakes and careened into the parking lot. Hell, even thinking about the woman made him forget what he was doing. Tess Abbot was definitely hands off.

#

She'd bought the thong underwear to spite Roman, only to find herself caught up by their arousing properties.

Troublesome man or not, she'd spent a restless night dreaming of her irksome contractor. Even a long day calling around for estimates on services and materials, couldn't keep her mind from wandering to Roman. No two ways about it, she wanted him enough to jeopardize her independence. Then again, if the attraction was purely sexual...

That last was what she was banking on when Roman's truck rumbled into the driveway. Tess turned from what she was doing at the stove with its steaming pots and toward the front door. Her father had often said, "The way to a man's heart is through his stomach."

Not that she was interested in Roman's heart as anything more than a means to a much lower part of his anatomy.

Outside, a truck door slammed. Tess smoothed her hands down the back of The Bargain Mart shorts. Just in case her father was as wrong about men's stomachs as he was about her, she'd dressed to appeal to that targeted male piece of anatomy. The pink short shorts and crop-top set from the Bargain Mart.

Roman walked in, plaid shirt slung over one shoulder, thermos caught between one big hand and a lean hip, and Bargain Mart bag dangling from his fingers. He stutter-stepped to a halt, his gaze fixed on her bare midriff. Bingo. Why had she bothered with kettles and hot water?

Then his gaze lifted to the stove behind her and he grimaced. "You're cooking?"

"Relax, St. John," she said. "It's spaghetti."

He raised an eyebrow at her.

"I can boil pasta."

He hung his shirt on the peg by the door, circled the table away from her, dropped his thermos by the sink, and stopped in front of the stove.

"The sauce smells...good," Roman said, his voice edged with astonishment.

"It should," she returned acidly. "It's yours."

Roman looked at her, that quizzical eyebrow raised once more.

"I found it in your freezer."

"In that case," he said, sounding far too relieved, "supper should be edible."

"Just go wash up," she muttered.

Roman tossed his bag of shorts on his bed then escaped into the bathroom. Slumping against the sink, he promptly suffered the pinch of an over-stimulated libido. He jerked back from the unyielding edge of the sink, scowled, and turned on the faucet.

The minute he'd spied Tess in that belly button baring, leg revealing, cotton-candy colored outfit, he'd wanted to throw her down across the kitchen table and nibble his way from one end of her to the other. Or maybe he'd have started with that ring piercing her belly button.

Yeah. He'd have started with that gleaming gold ring, then move to her creamy white skin. Aah, but in which direction to move? Upward to the underside of her sweet mounded breasts teasing him from the loose bottom of the cropped top or...downward? That path would be barred by the elastic waistband of the shorts...which he would chew through with the speed of a skill saw.

He tightened, filling the silk pouch, the caress of that slick fabric reminding him of her fingers around him. Roman groaned and shoved his hands into the steaming stream of water. Maybe a little blistered skin would keep his mind off Tess's skin...her very supple, very exposed skin. Smooth skin stretched across her flat stomach. Taut skin climbing from her polished red toenails to—

Roman groaned again. It wasn't his hands that needed blistering. But he hadn't the stomach for self-mutilation, especially not to the extent required to evict Tess Abbot from where she'd burrowed under his skin. For a woman who'd decreed sex between the two of them a bad idea, she sure wasn't making it easy for him to ignore her succulent body.

Or, maybe she didn't want to discourage him any longer. Maybe Tess Abbot was dishing up something besides a spaghetti dinner tonight. Maybe she was dishing up another dose of vengeance.

His arousal pressed against the zipper of his jeans. The discomfort of metal teeth reminded him of the pain she could cause his ego. He'd just have to muzzle his lust through supper.

He snorted. What he really wanted to muzzle was Tess' mouth.

Her delicious mouth with its ripe lips.

Roman groaned a third time and muttered at his reflection in the mirror above the sink, "Just get through supper without touching her. You can hold out that long."

And the rest of the evening?

He'd take a very cold shower after supper then lock himself in his office.

#

Tess wanted to dump the kettle of boiling spaghetti over Roman's head instead of into the colander in the kitchen sink. She wanted to turn to him where he sat at the head of the table and conk him on the head with the heavy pot.

She wanted to pour his precious spaghetti sauce into his lap.

Then lick up every last drop.

Tess struggled to stifle a moan. He'd insulted her cooking abilities and all but ignored her scant attire after that first reaction, and still she wanted him. She wanted him so badly she'd nearly bitten off her tongue to keep from saying what she really thought of his *supper should be edible* comment. Barbed comebacks were not conducive to seduction.

She ladled a healthy portion of sauce onto the spaghetti and placed the bowl of pasta on the table next to the tossed salad she'd prepared earlier. Roman was frowning at the salad.

"Something wrong?" she asked.

"I didn't know I had any croutons in the house."

"You didn't," she said sitting down opposite him. "I seasoned and toasted them from your old bread."

"You seasoned them?"

"I'm not totally inept in the kitchen."

He raised a skeptical eyebrow at her.

"I happen to mix a pretty mean salad."

"But the croutons..." He eyed the salad on the table between them, his brow puckered. "*What* did you season them with?"

Rat poison. That's what almost rolled off her tongue.

But she swallowed the comment. Seduction was tops on the menu for tonight, she reminded herself. Think sweet and non-confrontational. Think sexy, she silently prompted and smiled sweetly as she answered, "Garlic salt, sweet basil, and a little grated Parmesan."

He peered closely at the salad, his frown deepening. "Furry little things, aren't they?"

"For God's sake, Roman, they aren't poisoned." She snatched a crouton from the salad and popped it into her mouth, chewed, and swallowed. "Satisfied?"

He gave her a curious look.

Some seduction. At this rate, she'd still be chasing him around when they were using walkers. Maybe this was her subconscious' way of telling her to give up.

"Just eat your spaghetti before it gets cold," she grumbled.

His frown shifted to the bowl of sauce drenched pasta.

"Do I need to taste test the spaghetti to prove it's not poisoned either?" she asked.

"Hey, I'm not the one who brought up poison," he shot back.

"The hell you didn't. That look you gave the salad all but spelled out you thought it toxic."

"I was curious about the croutons."

"You were suspicious of the croutons. And now you're suspicious of the spaghetti. Let me show you how ridiculous you're being." She reached for the bowl.

He grabbed it off the table. "I'll eat it."

"I wouldn't dream of letting you take such a risk," she huffed back at him, standing and gripping the near rim of the bowl with both hands. "Not until I've taste-tested the blasted dish for you."

"I don't need you taste-testing anything for me." He tugged at the bowl. She tugged back. "Dammit woman, I ate your hamburgers without complaint."

"I knew you couldn't stay quiet about them forever," she howled, letting go of the bowl just as he jerked on it.

She'd never dreamed spaghetti could flip out of a bowl that easily, that spectacularly. But there they were, thin strands of pasta dripping with sauce flying through the air and landing in Roman's lap, the very lap she'd earlier fantasized dumping sauce into…and licking it up. How Freudian was this?

Roman, meanwhile, just sat there staring in disbelief at the mess in his lap. Then, with an ominous silence, he scooped up the tangle of noodles and deposited them back in their bowl.

"I'm sorry," she said, biting the insides of her cheeks not to laugh as she rounded the table toward him. "Let me help you clean up."

She began rubbing at his sauce stained lap with her napkin. He caught her by the wrist and stood. His chest rose and fell with each breath and, she swore, his nostrils even flared.

"I'll clean myself up," he said through tight lips, then released her and strode stiffly into the bathroom, slamming the door shut behind him.

Tess flinched. That wasn't quite the result she'd been going for. That wasn't even close to what she'd planned. Now what should she do?

In the bathroom, the water in the shower splashed on. The metallic scrape of the curtain hooks along the rod signaled when he'd stepped into the shower. He'd be naked in that shower…now. Wouldn't he be surprised if she walked in on him?

Surprised or aroused?

Or *angry*.

Only one way to find out.

Tess strode down the hall, opened the bathroom door with purpose, and tore back the shower curtain.

"Look here, Roman. You want it and I want it. We're both frustrated."

He gaped at her, steamy water spattering off the side of his head and sluicing down over his shoulder, his chest, his abdomen, his…

He dropped the washcloth he held between her gaze and his dangling assets. Oh yeah, they both wanted *it*.

She brought her gaze back up to his face and looked into his astonished eyes. "The only way we are going to end this frustration is to have sex. When you're ready, you know where to find me."

She released the shower curtain and walked out of the bathroom.

The closing door sent a current of cool air through the room, into the shower stall, and over Roman's wet body. It was like a slap to his ego. Or a wake-up call.

She had said they were both frustrated? Hell, Tess Abbot didn't know jack about frustration.

Frustration was looking into a woman's eyes and falling in love only to get your ears pinned back. Frustration was sleeping one flight below a temptress who slept in your t-shirt or less. Frustration was having your dick poised on the brink of hot, wet penetration only to be denied for lack of protection. He'd show her frustration.

He caught up to her half way to the kitchen, grabbed her by the upper arm and swung her against the wall. Before she could protest, he covered her mouth with his own, swallowing her surprised "Oh" and slipping his tongue between her parted teeth. Her body melted against his and her eyes drifted shut.

"Is this what you had in mind," he muttered against her lips, pinning her back against the wall with his wet body.

"It's a start," she purred, her fingers against the nape of his neck like tiny lightning strikes seeking ground on his water-beaded skin.

For a moment, he lost himself to the play of her small, taut tongue across his teeth. He lost himself in the lush curves she arched against his naked body—to the contact of her bare thigh to his naked sex. How easy it would be to strip away her skimpy shorts and whatever silk scrap of panty she wore beneath.

But he had something else in mind for Tess Abbot. He was going to teach her the meaning of frustration.

He clamped his hands over her hips and held her against the wall. He stroked her bare stomach with his thumbs—nudged the cool ring piercing her warm belly button. He stroked the ring again, circling it with one thumb. Circled it again and again. He wanted to know what that ring would feel like against the tip of his tongue—to taste it and find out if it tasted like her.

He wanted to taste her.

A low, warning growl rumbled in his throat. This wasn't supposed to be about pleasure. Not his. Not hers. This was supposed to be about teaching the woman who'd brought him to the boiling point only to deny him what that kind of frustration felt like.

He needed to tease her.

He stroked the bottom tines of her ribs. He stroked higher, beneath the loose bottom edge of the crop-top.

She squirmed beneath his touch.

He nudged the undersides of her breasts. Her moan buzzed against his lips, vibrated through his mouth, and reverberated straight into his primal core. He twitched against her thigh, realizing he'd sagged into her.

Not good. Not if he was going to make Tess Abbot suffer as he had.

Not when he needed to tame her.

He pulled back and removed his mouth from hers. He feathered kisses along the line of her jaw and nipped at the curve of her neck. She wriggled within the staying grip of his hands on her waist, straining against his restraint—struggling to lift her body against his.

She was close. Very close. Almost to the point where he'd been when she'd stopped them. But not quite close enough.

He moved one hand from her waist, moved it down her hip, across her thigh, and into the heat between her legs. Her body arched, tearing her mouth from his and pushing her body against his hand. As responsive as she was, he doubted he'd need do little more to bring her over the edge.

But, his intent wasn't to send her into the abyss of sexual release. If it were, he'd want to be with her, skin to skin. He'd want to be gripped by her contractions and drenched by her release.

He'd want to be inside her.

Heavy with his blood and his need, his sex throbbed between his legs.

He wanted to be inside her.

But, to give in to his need and join in her release was to lose.

Yet, to resist, to exact his vengeance by denying her, would be to deny himself. Something else niggled at him from deep in his soul. If he did conquer his own needs and extract his revenge, would he be able to look himself in the mirror tomorrow morning?

Roman went still and Tess met his conflicted gaze. There was a war waging inside him. She saw it in his eyes and in the pucker of his brow. She heard it in his ragged breaths—felt it in the tension of his muscles.

Continue or stop? That's the dilemma his body battled.

Strangely, she understood his conflict...though she suspected he struggled to stop for a different reason than she had the night they'd lain naked on the floor at the foot of her bed. She'd stopped them then because reason had prevailed.

But for Roman, the prevailing emotion warring with his passion was vengeance. She'd recognized it in the way he pinned her to the wall and the way he growled at her.

Anger.

Vengeance.

He wanted to pay her back for frustrating him. He wanted to leave her hungry for him. She almost welcomed his betrayal. It would make him like every other man in her life. It would kill this desire she felt for him.

It would make him...safe.

But the emotion in his eyes changed. The lines pinched around them telegraphed his decision before his ragged voice even spoke the words. "Do you still have those condoms?"

No. "In the dresser in my room."

He scooped her up in his arms and took the stairs two at a time. The thrill of it tickled Tess' stomach, and raised a trail of gooseflesh up her spine. What was wrong with her? This was what she'd intended to happen when she'd set out to seduce Roman. Wasn't it?

She buried her face against his shoulder. But, what if she was wrong? What if once would not be enough?

He dropped her beside the bed, spun toward the dresser, and began opening drawers, demanding, "Which one?"

Don't tell him. "Top right."

He faced her, condom box in hand. He was magnificent, standing there before her naked, damp, and fully aroused.

Last chance to stop this train wreck of an affair.

In one fluid movement, she peeled the crop-top off over her head and slid the shorts down her legs. Kicking the shorts aside, she stepped close to him and reached into the condom box.

"Let me help you," she said in a husky voice, so tremulous she almost didn't recognize herself.

His pupils flared, devouring his eyes, turning them a smoky shade of passion.

She tore open the foil wrapper, knelt before Roman, and placed the sheath on the tip of his cock. The condom box crushed in his fist and foil packets spilled out onto the floor.

"I better do that," he said in a tight voice, his

fingers replacing hers.

She rose and stroked his chest, his shoulders, his arms. He trembled with restraint. Against his own passion? Or against her?

"Roman," she whispered raggedly, "Are you sure—"

He cut her off with a kiss, a kiss that seemed to meld their lips together and send sparks down her throat, through her stomach, and into her womb. She opened her mouth wider, taking him as deep into her as she could, swallowing every passionate syllable he moaned and answering him with her own.

Beneath her hands, the muscles bunched across his shoulders, rippled down his spine, and contracted in his butt cheeks. His groan echoed through her mouth and into her soul. No one should have this much power over another. Not her over him. Not him over her.

But she loved the abrasive stroke of his broad, callused hands down her back. She loved the possessive wrap of his arms and the promise in his moans. She loved that he shuddered with need at her touch.

She hitched a leg over his hip, opening herself to him, inviting him closer. He caught her by the back of the knee, leaned down and nipped her throat.

She threw her head back and thrust her pelvis forward, begging for more. He bent and drew her nipple into his mouth, his suckling sending darts of pain and pleasure through her. So absorbed was she in his artful handling, she didn't notice him lowering her leg, not until her foot touched the floor.

"Please," she pleaded, trying to raise her foot again only to find he held her planted as firmly on two feet as a woman could be while a man trailed kisses down her stomach.

The tip of his tongue touched the ring in her belly button and a jolt as powerful as a lightning strike shot through her as though searching a route to exit. She knew where she wanted it to exit. She knew which part of Roman needed to connect with her in order for the path to be completed.

She struggled against the broad hands clamped over her hips, holding her in place while a masterful tongue explored the tiny gold ring and the terrain in which it had been planted. She gripped him by the shoulders to steady herself when he trailed feathery kisses across her abdomen and gasped approval when he hooked her leg over his shoulder.

One darting flick of his tongue and she crumpled against him. He lifted her onto the bed and finished the kiss he'd begun. Then he knelt between her legs and thrust himself inside her, at last bringing to ground the lightning bolts of pleasure zigzagging through her body.

#

In the first tentative grays of false dawn, Tess woke in Roman's arms, sated and deliciously sore. Roman had proven to be a thorough lover, not once, not twice, but three times.

The first time had been hot and frenzied. The second, they'd awakened on top of the covers in a tangle of limbs, still hungry for each other. But, playful this time, they'd wound up tumbling to the floor when reaching for the spilled condoms. Taking the dominant position, she'd ministered as thoroughly to him as he had to her the first time.

She purred with satisfaction and snuggled into the cradle of his body. God he felt good pressed against the length of her back. All that hot, hard flesh.

He stirred against her, making her body twitch in the most distracting of places. She wasn't going to let him sleep if he kept moving against her like that.

But four times in one night? What could they possibly do that was more sating than their third love making session, the one that had been tender and sweet? It was more cuddling than fireworks and, in some ways, the most satisfying of all.

...And the most unsettling, now that she thought about it.

One of Roman's calloused hands slid from her hip and splayed across her belly. Possessive? For a woman who'd sworn never again to allow herself to be possessed by any man, she liked far too much the notion of belonging to Roman. She squeezed her eyes shut, finally putting into words what had freaked her out about him the first time she'd looked into his eyes.

Soul mate. That's what she'd seen when she'd opened The Castle door to him the day they first met face-to-face. And soul mate equaled love. One did not seduce a soul mate and expect to walk away unscathed. She'd known that all along. That's why she'd held him at bay with terse words and petty complaint...until last night. She clearly hadn't thought her choice through as thoroughly as she thought she had.

Roman's breath stirred against her neck. She wasn't going to figure this out as long as she stayed in his arms, relishing his breath on her neck and tingling to his touch.

She eased out from under his arm and out of the bed where they'd made love throughout the night.

Made love. She stifled a groan. Why couldn't it have been just great sex?

That had been the plan. A night of great sex and

the itch would be gone. What a fool she'd been.

She slipped into The Bargain Mart robe and fled down the steps.

The scene that greeted her when she turned on the kitchen light was little better than what she ran from. The meal they'd left forgotten when passion had taken over covered the kitchen table like a battlefield post skirmish.

Cinching the robe closed, she went about picking up the mess. Activity always helped her think. But, swiping the spilled spaghetti from tabletop into garbage bag reminded her how shocked Roman looked when the pasta landed in his lap—of how she'd had all she could do to keep from laughing. Not so funny now that she realized sex hadn't been the answer to her itch.

She dumped the wilted salad into the bag and loaded the dishwasher, nagged by the one question that hung over her like Damocles' sword. Could she and Roman keep this conflagration of an attraction confined to the bedroom?

With dampened dishcloth in hand, she turned to the table. Through the open door of Roman's bedroom, the corner of his bed was visible—his *marriage* bed. Roman St. John wanted a wife to keep his house and to be the mother of his children. She wasn't that woman. That was the problem. She couldn't be what he needed in his life without losing who she was.

A stair step squeaked. She stilled. Roman reached around her, taking the cloth from her hand and enclosing her in his embrace before she could answer her own question.

"We could have cleaned this up together in the morning," he said.

Together? Could he be that partner oriented? Or was he courting her? In her experience men tended to say, even do, whatever it took to get a woman to put on his ring. But Roman had proven himself a man of his word.

Tentatively, she laid her head against his shoulder. "What are we going to do now?"

He tossed the rag onto the table, turned her, and brushed his lips across hers. "How's that for starters?"

A kinder, gentler Roman was not what she needed when she was trying to figure out if there was a way for them to both get what they wanted. Better for her if Roman was snapping and snarling at her.

No. His sparring with her had acted more like foreplay than anything else. Six weeks plus of foreplay. No wonder their fiasco of a dinner had ended in the best sex of her life.

She groaned and pressed her face into his shoulder.

Roman's arms tightened around her. "Tess? Is there a problem?"

She rolled her head back and forth. "Having sex was supposed to have ended the frustration." *Not make me want more.*

She could almost hear the smile stretch across his lips. "It did a pretty good job for me. I'm not nearly as wired as I was before. Didn't it work that way for you?"

"We're too different," she said.

"We're supposed to be different," he murmured against her temple. "That's what enables a man's body and a woman's body to fit together."

"We want different things," she argued, trying to extricate herself from his arms.

"Just tell me what you want," he whispered,

brushing his lips across her ear. "I'll be happy to try again."

"It wasn't a good idea last Friday night and it still isn't a good idea."

He nipped her earlobe. "You're the one who charged into my shower telling me it was the only thing we could do."

"I was wrong. There. I said it. Just the thing you've been waiting weeks to hear from me. I was wrong."

He laughed a deep heady, nerve-provoking laugh. "Then let me show you all that's right between us, Princess."

He reached under the satin robe.

"This isn't about sex," she protested.

Still, her insides turned liquid in response to his touch. She wanted to enjoy more of what they had shared through the night. But, there were issues to settle.

"Roman—"

He stopped her with a kiss.

"We need to talk," she muttered against his lips.

"Shhh," buzzed his command against her mouth.

"But—"

He pulled her against his hard, naked body and backed her into the table. The chilly Formica made her jump against him. His resulting moan reverberated clear down her throat to the center of her being. Roman St. John was every bit as intoxicating as she'd feared he would be.

And she was drunk with him. Drunk with the feel of his hard angles and planes pressed the length of her body. Drunk with his soul-devouring kiss.

Drunk with her need for him.

He picked her up by the waist and deposited her

on the table, whispering against the corner of her mouth, "Am I getting it right?"

No! Yes!

She clung to a sanity fast slipping away beneath the sweep of his thumbs across her abdomen.

"Roman, wait," she breathed even as her legs spread to accommodate him.

He stood between her thighs and smiled down at her. "Did I start on the wrong end?"

"No," she exhaled before catching herself. "I mean—"

"Maybe you'd have preferred I start with your hungry-for-attention breasts?" He palmed her through the sateen fabric, making her ache all the more for him.

"I thought you found my breasts lacking," she countered in an attempt to cool his ardor…and hers. Anything to get him to stop so she could think things out.

"I never called your breasts lacking." He nudged aside a lapel and fit his lips around one straining peak, his breath hot against her cool skin.

She gasped, "When I told you I did your laundry, you asked if I wanted a medal or a chest to pin it on."

He chuckled against her nipple and nipped her playfully before raising his face to hers. "That was a foolish thing for me to say."

She was only vaguely aware of his hand at her waist loosening the tie that held the front of her robe together. The cool, pre-dawn air invading the house shivered across her bared skin, while his palm cupped her breast in a fiery caress.

He gazed down at her through passion-drugged eyes. "The truth is, Princess, you're a perfect fit."

He pressed her down on the table, his mouth

replacing his hand on her breast, her stomach…between her legs. She should fight him off. But his artful tongue wreaked havoc with her resistance. Besides, it wasn't the sex that was the problem.

The problem was… The problem was…

Oh hell, who could think about problems with such a delicious heat rippling through her?

Warning tapped against her skull. But who could listen to silly noises in her head when an artful lover played a rhapsody between your thighs?

But the warning was persistent. It scratched at her ears almost as though it came from outside her.

Nearing the optimum moment of no return, she heard the whimper. Faint but plaintive enough to reach beyond her body and touch her soul.

Tess levered herself onto her elbows, canted her head toward the door, and listened. There it was again, scratching.

She grabbed Roman by the hair and hauled his head up.

"What?" he gasped.

"There's something at the door."

"Not into exhibitionism?" he teased, wagging his eyebrows at her.

She pushed him back, sat up, and demanded, "Listen."

"Probably just a branch," he said, nuzzling her throat.

"At the door on the porch?" she insisted, swatting him away and scrambling off the table.

"Tess, wait," he called after her. "It could be a skunk."

Too late. She already had the door open.

CHAPTER ELEVEN

"It's a dog," she said, dropping to her knees beside the German shepherd belly down on Roman's front porch. "And he's hurt."

Roman peeked over Tess' shoulder.

"Call the animal ER," she commanded, hovering over the animal.

Roman took a stiff step toward the wall phone.

"And turn on the porch light," she commanded.

Roman pivoted, flicked on the light, and glanced again over Tess' shoulder. Her hands stroked the big shepherd, his sides puffing in and out with shallow breaths.

No, not stroked, examined. The woman he'd called a pampered princess knelt bare-knee on his damp porch, probing for injuries on an animal big enough to eat her face off. He opened his mouth to warn her; but the dog seemed relaxed beneath her gentle hands and soft, soothing tone. His baby brother had that kind of knack with animals. His mother had it with children. His sister had it with both. He'd never considered Tess had an ounce of empathy for either.

Though, there had been that one time a couple kids came to The Castle selling candy bars for a school project. He and each member of the crew had bought a bar from each kid. Tess had bought ten...from each kid. Twenty candy bars at a buck a pop.

He'd have bet she'd have chased them off with

her broom, or invited them inside and popped them into the oven Hansel and Gretel style, not sent them skipping off with empty candy boxes and stuffed money pouches. And she'd smiled after them, amused by their excitement.

"Dog emergency room," Tess prompted over her shoulder.

Roman jerked into motion but, some of his blood having finally located his brain, he stopped halfway to the phone. "We don't have an animal emergency room."

Tess raised her head and peered blankly at him. "What do you people do if you have an animal emergency after hours?"

"Call the after-hours number for the Veterinary Clinic," he said, heading to the phone.

Since when had he stopped being the level-headed one? Since when had anyone had to order him around in an emergency he quizzed himself as he looked up the after-hours number for the animal clinic? He'd always been the decisive one, he reasoned as he dialed the number. The calm and collected big brother. The "Family Patriarch in Training" as his sister had often teased him. Yet, Tess had been as take charge and as level-headed as he'd ever been in the middle of an emergency. And Jake, the true oldest brother, was stone-cold cool in emergencies.

The veterinarian's sleep thick voice answered on the third ring. Fifteen minutes later, dressed and the dog laid out on his truck's bench seat, they pulled into the parking lot of the Pine Mountain Animal Clinic. Dr. DeBaker had already arrived and had the clinic unlocked and lights on. He met Roman at the passenger side door of the truck as he opened it.

"He reacts when I touched his hip," Tess said from the floor where she'd crouched the entire trip, soothing the dog and keeping him from sliding around. Tess, whom he'd have bet his last dollar, would have been the last person to scuff up her knees over a stray dog.

The two men carried the dog into the clinic on the makeshift litter Roman had cut from a piece of plywood, as Tess explained how they'd found the dog on "our porch."

Our porch. They were in the middle of an emergency and he was noticing things like Tess calling his porch *ours*. Noticing it and liking it.

"We think he was hit by a car," Tess elaborated as the vet palpated the dog's abdomen.

"There were skid marks in front of the house," Roman added.

The dog whimpered. She stroked his head, her tone immediately soothing. Tess Abbot gone all motherly was about the last thing he expected to ever see.

She swiped a tear from her eye. "How could anyone hit this beautiful animal then just drive away?"

A man had to love a woman who wept for a dog.

Love? Did he love Tess Abbot?

#

The vet ordered them out of the exam room while he took X-rays. Tess used the time to call the phone number she'd gotten off the dog's tags and found a frantic owner who'd been searching most of the night for her dog.

"The owner's on her way," Tess informed Roman when she hung up the phone in the vet's reception area.

"You're really good in an emergency," he said.

"I told you I could take care of myself."

"This is beyond taking care of yourself, Princess."

Was he going to call what she did mothering? Her nerves were too frazzled and her mind too uncertain yet to deal with that issue. Hell, she wasn't even ready to call what was going on between them a relationship.

"It was pretty brave of you to take on an injured dog." Roman said.

Brave was a better topic to deal with…even if she was not brave enough to confess that she'd seen soul mate in his eyes the first time they'd met face-to-face. She hugged her arms across her stomach.

"You look cold," he said, draping his jacket over her shoulders. He stood there a moment, the lapels of the jacket caught in his fingers, looking at her.

Silently, she begged him not to push for more. Not now. Not at this moment. If he pushed now, she'd crumble. She'd collapse into his arms and vow to make herself into everything he wanted. And later, when she was thinking clearly again, she would resent him for that decision. She was a woman who had no intention of putting her brain in neutral for any man. Not even a man who was a thorough lover and compassionate human being.

The vet motioned them back into the exam room where he had the X-ray already up on the lighted viewer. The dog's leg was broken, but not badly. The dog would be fine.

But would she?

Roman looped an arm around her shoulder, pulled her against his side, and smiled down at her. "You did good, Princess. I'm going to have to reward you, aren't I?"

A frisson of heat zipped through her. She knew exactly what kind of reward he had in mind…just the kind she craved now that she'd sampled the man. Damn, but she wanted him.

Then why not have him? Making love to the most glorious man on earth didn't make her dependent on him. It didn't even need to be forever.

#

Tess pulled into Roman's driveway, parked the car, and trotted up to the house. Aside from having forgotten her notebook, life was good, great even. Clean up at The Castle had moved along well in the week since she'd moved into Roman's bed. The wood floors hadn't been ruined by all the water poured on the fire and only the second floor ceilings and walls and the third floor bonus room would need new sheetrock. She could thank Roman for calling in a favor with the water extraction team and getting them working immediately. The sprayed-in insulation she'd chosen didn't absorb water and that had saved her from having to rip out a lot more sheetrock to replace insulation. Fortunately there'd been little carpeting to tear-out and all of Aunt Honey's antique furnishing on the lower floors survived. To top it all off, there was great sex no strings attached.

Somewhere deep inside her, something told her there were always strings attached. But she refused to listen. She was happy, even if she'd had to interrupt her work at The Castle because she'd left her notebook back at Roman's.

She was on the brink of the stairway to the second floor when voices coming from the back drew her to the screen door. Outside, Roman pulled a length of lumber from beneath the deck with the help of a boy who couldn't be more than three or four. Wheat hued hair poked out from beneath the yellow, child-sized hard hat. Add a toy tool belt and he was a miniature of the man. He had to be Roman's nephew.

Roman held the board up to his eye, sighting the length of it. "Good and straight," he said.

The boy held a shorter board likewise to his eye and declared, "Good and straight."

"Do you remember our measurement?" Roman asked.

The boy recited a number. Roman smiled. "Good job."

The child beamed. Tess couldn't help but smile.

With dual tape-measures, the boy's a smaller version of Roman's, they both measured the board and made pencil marks. "We'll make our cut now," Roman said, slipping on his safety glasses. "You know what to do when I cut."

The child put on a tiny pair of goggles and stepped behind Roman as Roman picked up a skill saw and braced the board across two saw horses.

This is the kind of father Roman was going to be, protecting, educating, nurturing. The wine of the saw died off as Roman finished his cut and Tess' smile faded. What was she doing rolling around between the sheets with a man who had a life plan that had no room in it for her?

Roman handed the cut board to the kid, hoisted him onto his shoulders, and headed off across the yard. She ached to have had such a father—ached to know she'd never have what that little boy had in Roman. She raised a hand to the screen as though she might be able to feel their camaraderie through the mesh—capture what she'd missed in her own youth.

"You must be Tess," a sweet female voice said

behind her, making her jump.

The petite blonde held out a hand, "I'm Dixie, Roman's sister."

"Y-yes," Tess said, accepting the curvy blonde's hand. "I recognize you from the pictures Roman has around the house."

Dixie's curls shuddered with the shake of her head. "What? He hasn't talked about me?"

"Ah. Some. It sounds like he's talked about me, though."

Dixie's curled lips lifted further. "Some."

It was clear he'd told his sister a whole lot more than *some,* not that his sister was hiding the fact. She struck her as a very open person and one with wicked sense of humor that went right along with those happy face pajamas she'd given Roman.

"It was nice meeting you," Tess said, shifting away from the screen door. "I just stopped by to pick up something I forgot here."

"Don't leave."

Tess paused. "I don't want to intrude on your family time."

"Nonsense," Dixie said, looping her arm through Tess' and turning them both toward the screen door. "You're not intruding at all."

The back door squeaked open and Roman glanced up from the board he was nailing to the frame bolted into place in the lowest crux of an oak. Arm in arm, Dixie and Tess approached, Dixie grinning, Tess looking apprehensive. He sighed. Good or bad, the two had to meet sometime.

"Look who I found watching you from the back door," Dixie said.

Tess blanched as though she'd been caught with her hand in the proverbial cookie jar. "I heard talking and came to check…"

He gave Tess a reassuring smile and nodded her closer. "Come. We could use an architect's input on this job."

"Yeah," the child said, pausing with toy hammer in hand. "We could use an archt'ict on this job."

Roman placed a hand on the child's shoulder. "This is my number one man on the job, my nephew Benjamin. Ben, this is my friend Tess."

The kid held his free hand up to Tess. "Hello, Miss Tess."

Tess released herself from Dixie, squatted in front of the boy, and took his hand. "Nice to meet you, Benjamin."

"Ev'rybody calls me Ben. They used to call me Benj. But-but I'm too big for that now."

"Okay, Ben. So, what do you and your uncle want this architect to do about your job?"

Ben peered up at Roman, his big, round eyes questioning.

"We can always use an architect to check our construction, make sure it's done properly," Roman said. "Can never be too safe when building a treehouse."

"Never be too safe," Ben mimicked.

Tess nodded.

"I'll leave you three to the construction work," Dixie said. "I've got groceries to put away."

Tess was under the platform inspecting struts before Dixie was halfway to the house.

"You're taking this job seriously," Roman said, joining her.

"Like you said, "can't be too careful with a structure built off the ground, especially for a little tyke."

"That's why it's so low," Roman said.

"What a tyke?" Ben asked.

Backing out from under the treehouse, Tess raised a questioning eyebrow at Roman, clearly uncertain how to answer without wounding Ben's pride. Roman smiled at her as he straightened and held the flat of his hand half a foot above Ben's head. "A tyke is anyone whose head doesn't touch my hand."

Ben jumped, trying to touch his head to Roman's hand.

"I not a tyke," Ben said.

"No, you're not," Tess said, squatting and lifting Ben until his head touched Roman's hand.

Ben giggled and Tess lifted eyes full of devilment at Roman. He liked when she teased him. But, he liked even more how naturally she interacted with Ben, letting him take her hand and lead her around to where the ladder attached to the treehouse.

"I like that you angled it and made the treads flat," she said. "Even if I was wearing my heels, I could climb a ladder like this."

Ben's grin widened and Roman's heart swelled.

"You goin' ta help us?" Ben asked.

"If you'll let me."

Ben's expression turned serious. "You gotta wear a hard hat on a job site."

Tess looked like she was fighting to keep from laughing but managed a sober," Got it covered," then trotted off around the corner of the house. A car door opened and closed and she reappeared, hard hat atop her head.

Ben's mouth popped open and he looked at his uncle with huge eyes. "She has her own hard hat! I gotta tell mama."

Roman laughed.

"Where's Ben going in such a hurry?" Tess asked as she approached Roman.

"Suffice it to say, you having your own hard hat raised you to a very elite status with the kid."

"I'm honored."

"You should be. So far, only his uncles have made that club."

She blinked. "Wow. Am I going to have to top a hard hat to stay in that club?"

"Nah," Roman said, slinging an arm around her shoulders and drawing her close. "Once you're in you're in forever."

"Forever, huh?"

There was an odd note in her voice. But, before he could decide whether it was wistful or apprehensive, Ben came running back, all little boy hoots and hollers. Back to nailing up boards with Ben, Roman tried to make eye contact with Tess. But she seemed off in her own world, studying the wall of the treehouse facing his house. He was just about to send Ben for more nails so he could talk to Tess when she asked him the last question he'd have expected from her.

"Can I borrow your truck?"

"Sure. Keys are in the ignition."

"Be back in a few minutes," she said and sprinted off toward the driveway.

Dixie appeared at his elbow, a plate of sandwiches and pitcher of lemonade in hand. "Where's Tess going?"

"I don't know."

"She's coming back, isn't she?"

"She better. She took my truck."

Roman, Dixie, and Ben were finishing their

sandwiches on the treehouse platform when Tess returned, dragging a curved, yellow, semi-tubular fiberglass object behind her. Roman hopped off low platform and met her.

"What's that?" he asked.

"What that?" mimicked Ben from the platform.

Grinning, Tess braced the tubular end up against the treehouse wall and turned it so everyone could see the open end nearest the ground.

"A slide," hooted Ben.

"On the way here this morning," she said to Roman, "I noticed one of your neighbors dismantling an old play set."

Roman examined the bolt holes at the top of the slide. "No cracks or brittleness. Looks to be in good shape."

"That's what I wanted to check out before I said anything," Tess said.

Ben whooped. "Can I slide down it?"

"After we've attached it to the treehouse," Tess said then looked at Dixie. "Providing your mother approves of the addition."

"Please, please," Ben chimed.

Dixie stroked her son's blond head. "Uncle Roman and Miss Tess are the experts here. If they think it's safe, it's a go."

Ben beamed. "Miss Tess is an arch'tect. She'll make sure it's safe."

Roman sidled up alongside Tess and tipped his head close to hers. "You trying to outdo his uncles?"

Tess squinted at him. "What do you mean?"

"I think you just topped having your own hard hat."

#

Tess' laughter filled Roman's heart as they

devoured the dinner Dixie had cooked for them. They shared a lot of the same likes and dislikes…and values as judged by their phone and text exchanges in the weeks leading up to actually meeting. The intensity of their attraction could be measured by the sparks that flew between them in the weeks working together even as Tess tried her damnedest to keep him at bay with her shrew impersonation…and their lovemaking since. But, what made their relationship feel real was moments like these, sitting around a table eating, laughing, sharing. He loved this side of Tess best of all. He loved her.

But that was his heart talking…and his libido. He was a man who planned his moves and depended on facts to make decisions.

"I can hardly wait to tell Aunt Honey that the best Chicken Marsala I've ever eaten I ate at a picnic table in someone's back yard," Tess said, rubbing her stomach. "Not that Honey will be all that surprised. She always said a person will find the best of anything in the least expected places."

"You think I could add it to the Farmhouse menu then?" Dixie asked.

"You could add it to the menu of a five star restaurant," Tess answered, rising from the bench beside Roman. "Excuse me, but I ate so much I think I'll explode if I don't move."

She began to gather the empty dishes.

"I'll take of those," Dixie said, starting to rise.

Tess flattened a hand at her. "Stay. Relax. You did all the cooking."

"You helped my son and his uncle build a treehouse."

"You have a long drive ahead of you," Tess countered.

"I give," Dixie said, settling back on the picnic table bench.

When the screen door shut behind Tess, Roman looked at his sister. "What do you think of her?"

"I like her," Ben piped from beside his mother.

Dixie and Roman exchanged glances and Dixie sent Ben off with his cup to *help Miss Tess in the kitchen.*

"Now that little ears are out of hearing range," Dixie said, "Is she the one?"

Roman picked at a bread crumb on the table. "I want to think so."

"But?"

He crushed the crumb between his fingers and looked across the table at his sister. "The facts are she's all career. I don't think marriage is in her plans."

Dixie chuckled. "Dear practical Roman. Love isn't all about facts."

Roman sighed.

"Sounds like you two need to do some talking," Dixie said.

"I don't even know if she wants kids and you know how important family is to me." He frowned. "I think I'm afraid to find out."

Dixie placed a hand on Roman's arm. "I doubt you have as much to worry about as you think. When I came up behind her, caught her watching you and Ben through the screen door, I saw a woman full of longing."

#

They stood on the porch waving good-bye to Dixie and Ben as Dixie backed out of Roman's driveway.

"You're a natural with Ben," Roman said.

"Surprised?" Tess asked without looking at him.

"Yes and no. You went all motherly on that injured dog."

Dixie's vehicle trundled off into the sunset and Tess faced Roman. "He was helpless."

"Yeah," Roman said, leaning a shoulder against a porch support. "And those girls who came selling chocolate bars at The Castle, why'd you buy every piece of candy they had? They weren't helpless."

She hitched herself up onto the railing. "I'm always happy to encourage female entrepreneurs."

"And here I just bought their candy because they were cute?"

Tess leveled on him a chastening look. "Girls should never rely on their looks for gain. I bought what I did because they had a good sales pitch."

"Sure," he said, not even trying to hide his amusement. "And the reason for your charm around little boys?"

She gave him a crooked smile. "They grow up to be handsome big boys."

He snickered. She shrugged. "I'm not without some experience around children. I have nieces and nephews."

"So you have siblings," Roman said, his interest heightening.

Her smile slipped and she swung her legs over the railing so she sat facing away from the house, breaking eye contact. "Two older sisters."

"Are you close with them?" he asked, figuring he already knew the answer, his own grin fading.

"They followed our father's life-plan for daughters. Though neither of them married an architect into the family to partner in the family business."

The daddy issue makes a return appearance.

"Was that supposed to be your job?"

She stared off into the darkening woods. "It seems so."

"But you didn't do it."

"I almost did."

"What happened?"

The near corner of her mouth flattened. "I realized Harry was a parasite before it was too late."

The muscles across Roman's shoulders tensed. He wanted to go to her, take her in his arms as he had the night she'd confessed about the boy who'd left her to drown. But he held back. "What'd he do?"

"Passed off one of my designs as his own," she said through tight lips.

"Your father must have gone ballistic when you told him."

A muscle popped at the hinge of her jaw. "The design won the firm a major low income housing contract from the government."

"Your father must have been very proud of you," he said even though a sheen of moisture in her eyes warned him otherwise.

"The only thing my father commended me on was backing my man by supplying him with the plan. He said Harry was the salesman who sold the project to the government, that no one was going to take me seriously. He said it was a woman's place to support her man."

"That doesn't sound right."

"It wasn't," she said, blinking and turning her face away. "That's why I left the family firm and my father."

And came to the Upper Peninsula of Michigan to start her career over, he thought.

"He wouldn't even have that firm if it wasn't for

my mother's family money," she went on, blankly staring toward the road in front of the house.

Roman frowned, but said nothing. He knew when to let a woman talk.

"When they married, my mother handed over everything she had to him. He's never even given her credit for setting him up in business. Then he had the gall to blame her for not giving him a son." A tear slid down her cheek.

Roman straightened from the porch upright, went to her, and placed his hands on her shoulders.

She swiped the tear away. "Don't you dare feel sorry for me St. John."

"I'm not," he said, massaging her knotted muscles. "Just giving you some of the TLC you deserve."

She leaned back against him. "You're a good man, Roman St. John. The kind a woman can lean on."

"That's how a man should be with the woman he cares about." He felt the hitch in her breathing through his hands on her shoulders. He wanted her to say she cared about him, too. He wanted to know if she saw a future between them that went beyond the bedroom.

"Enough talk about my dysfunctional family," she said, turning beneath his hands, forcing him to release her. "You've got a family of rather diverse interests and Ben seems to know every one of his uncles quite well in spite of how spread out you all are."

So she wasn't ready to commit.

"We keep close however we can," he said. "Phoning, emailing, texting."

She put her back to the porch upright and drew a

leg up onto the railing. "What's Dixie's story? How'd a woman who can cook a five star Chicken Marsala wind up selling food out of a farmhouse?"

"She's always wanted to run a little restaurant. Was a natural in the kitchen, so she went to school for restaurant management."

"And set up shop in a farmhouse?"

A breeze rifled through Tess' loose locks, his fingers itching to do likewise. But he knew now was not the time. Instead, he leaned into the post Tess sat against. "Eventually."

Tess peered over her shoulder at him. "There's a world of innuendo in that word. What's missing?"

He met her gaze, looked her deep in the eye, willing her not to take what he was about to say the wrong way. "She fell in love and married before she could set her dream in motion."

Tess shook her head. "Love ruins the best laid plans."

He frowned. "It doesn't have to."

"Says the guy whose family keeps in touch via phone, email, and texting."

"Actually, the guy she married was able to fast track her dream. He came from money. He adored her. So he bought her a restaurant."

She tipped her head back against the post. "Why doesn't that sound like a happily ever after?"

"The short of it is, Michael died in a car accident last December."

Tess dropped her foot to the porch floor and looked up at him. "I'm so sorry."

"On top of that, the restaurant never really caught on and Mike's father fought Dixie for custody of Ben."

"That's awful."

"She spent just about everything she had fighting to keep Ben, losing the restaurant in the battle."

Tess stood and paced to the end of the porch, shaking her head. "She's so upbeat, so bubbly. I'd never guess she'd been through so much."

"Dixie is the eternal optimist. Give her lemons…"

"And she'll make lemonade."

He smiled, liking that she could finish his sentences. "You got it."

"How'd she wind up turning a farmhouse into a restaurant?"

He strode the distance between them, stopped at her side facing the woods. "Our grandmother was widowed and in failing health. She needed live-in help."

"So, good hearted Dixie volunteered."

"It was a mutually beneficial arrangement. Gran got the live-in help she needed. Dixie and Ben got a roof over their heads. Gran was already selling ice cream, baked goods, and preserves from the front parlor. Dixie expanded into the dining room and back parlor and now serves breakfast and lunch five days a week."

She smiled slyly up at him. "From a restaurant quality kitchen built by you."

"All us brothers got together a few months ago to build the kitchen and partition the private quarters from the public rooms. How'd you know I was even involved in that addition?"

"You should password protect your computer."

"I've got nothing to hide."

Her smile faded. "So it seems. You've been pretty clear about what you want out of life all along. A family."

His chest tightened. This was as direct as she'd ever gotten with a topic that could include them both. Dared he hope?

He drew a deep breath and ventured, "I want what my parents had. How about you, Tess? Isn't there anything you want outside a career?"

She dropped her chin, tilting her face from his scrutiny. "I've been focused on becoming a topnotch architect for so long—fought for it so long, I haven't given any thought to what else I might want."

He placed a hand on her shoulder. She stiffened.

"All this fresh air has worn me out," she said. "I think I'll hit the sack early tonight."

With that she turned, gave him a light kiss on the lips, and headed into the house. He watched her through the screen door walk past his bedroom and climb the steps. He thought about following her into the house, up the steps, and into her bed. But he'd gotten the message in her kiss, in how abruptly she'd ended their conversation. Tess Abbott had some things to think through and a wise man would give her the time and space to do just that.

CHAPTER TWELVE

Roman trotted up the front steps of The Castle. His sister was right. He and Tess needed to talk. The necessary conversation had only just started last evening after Dixie and Ben had left. Then Tess had left before he got up this morning and he'd been stuck all morning at his job site.

He climbed The Castle stairs to the second floor master bedroom where he found Tess bent over a sooty packing carton, her delectable backside waving in the air. It was almost enough to make him forget about any discussion. He gave a low whistle of appreciation that brought her upright and facing him.

Soot smudged her brow and dotted her chin. She'd be horrified if she could see herself. He thought she looked adorable and couldn't help but tease her. "That box from the attic?"

"It's one of the few that survived."

"And you removed it from an attic we aren't even supposed to go into," he said with mock authority.

"And aren't you supposed to be at work?" she said, straightening, a twinkle in her eye.

"Even the boss gets a lunch hour," he replied, leaning into the doorframe, thoroughly enjoying the view.

She raised her eyebrows at him. "And you came here thinking I'd feed you?"

He produced an exaggerated mock shiver. "Not unless Mrs. Antonetti has sent over something."

She snatched a pillow off the bed and flung it at

him. He boxed it aside with one hand.

"I've got a better idea," she said, smiling devilishly. She strode up to him, caught him by the belt buckle, and drew him toward the bed. "How much time do you have?"

"I'm the boss. I have as much time as I need," he said, giving in to his libido. They could talk tonight.

"Shouldn't the boss set a good example?" she teased, deftly unbuckling his belt.

He laughed and caught her up in his arms and kissed her hard. They were like teenagers, tearing at each other's clothes, not bothering to remove anything more than what was necessary to allow them access to the most intimate parts of each other's bodies. When he reached up to remove his hard hat, she murmured against his ear, "Leave it on."

They started on the bed amidst the piles of bedding just back from the cleaners. But soon found themselves dumped on the floor between the bed and the wall, tangled in a quilt and each other's limbs.

They laughed and teased each other to delicious heights, Roman with his pants snagged around his ankles and the yellow hard hat askew atop his head. Tess beneath him with her soot smudged face and—

A throaty cough cut through the room. Roman rose onto his knees and peered across the mounded bed to find a barrel-chested man in a hard hat all but filling the bedroom doorway. Every protective nerve in his body went on alert and he demanded, "Who the hell are you?"

"I'm the Fire Marshal," the big man returned. "Who the hell are you?"

"Ooops," Tess said. "Did I forget to tell you the Fire Marshal called this morning to tell me he'd be coming by this afternoon?"

Roman's confrontational sneer crumpled and an expression of abject wretchedness replaced it. He looked every bit the hormone charged teenager caught in the back seat of a car with his pants down. Tess' laughter started in her diaphragm, jerky spasms of it that butted her body against Roman's.

He hissed for her to be silent and introduced himself to the Fire Marshall…without standing or emerging from behind the bed of course. "Roman St. John. I'm the contractor."

She couldn't see the man who'd interrupted them, but his voice boomed through the room. "I'll be on the third floor checking out the fire area." Then, in a less brusque tone the Fire Marshal added, "Good to see you're using protection."

Roman blanched and the Fire Marshall added a droll, "I was referring to the hard hat."

Laughter burst from Tess. Roman stuffed the edge of the quilt in her face…which only provoked her to higher levels of mirth.

When the Fire Marshall was out of sight, Roman lifted the quilt from Tess' face and frowned at her. "I was trying to protect your reputation."

She shifted beneath him, her body racked with a new wave of laughter. "*My* reputation?"

His frown twisted into a scowl. "Yes. Your reputation. Your virtue."

"Virtue?" She snorted. "I think my virtue was compromised a long time ago." If he'd had his belt in its proper place, she'd have grabbed him by that. She grabbed the next most prominent thing sticking out.

Roman buckled over her, croaking out, "You've got a Fire Marshal in your attic."

She nibbled at his lips, murmuring, "But one contractor in my bedroom trumps ten Fire Marshals in the attic."

"He could come back," Roman managed between kisses and tugging at his pants.

"What's the matter, St. John? You not into the excitement of getting caught?" She stroked him, eliciting a groan.

"One thrill a day is enough for me."

"One a day is enough, huh? Since when?"

"I'm talking about getting caught."

"You weren't concerned about getting caught the night the dog showed up on our doorstep," she purred, wrapping her fingers around him.

He jerked and sank back on his heels. "If you don't knock it off, I'll tell everyone you have a hard hat fetish."

"While you're at it—" She curled into a sitting position and hooked her fingers through his belt loops. "—Tell them I like tool belts on a man, too, tool laden and slung low on the hips."

He slapped her hands away, pulled his jeans up all the way this time and snapped them shut.

"Yep," she said, rising to her knees and unsnapping him as he zipped up.

He caught her by the wrists and held her hands out of reach of his pants. "Don't you think the Fire Marshal got a good enough look at us the first time he caught us?"

"He didn't see anything."

"He saw enough to know what we were doing."

"We are two consenting adults. We weren't doing anything illegal."

"I'm just not into showing my woman to the world rolling around bedroom floors, half undressed, playing out sex fantasies with a man in a hard hat."

She raised an eyebrow at Roman. "Your

woman?"

Roman forced a hopeful smile. "Yeah. My woman. What do you say to that?"

What should she say? Don't start getting all possessive with me? Or, yes, make me yours? Which did she want?

His thumbs stroked the pulse points of her wrists, sending delicious ripples up her arms, down through her chest, straight to her—

"Don't you want me looking out for your virtue, Princess?"

"That sounds like the sort of thing a man would do for the mother of his children," she murmured, swaying in time with those sweeping thumbs. She was in heaven and she wanted never to leave.

His brilliant blue eyes gleamed. "Would you like to be the mother of my children, Tess?"

Tess went still. Children? His? Was he proposing?

He gave a tight chuckle. "Hey, Princess, quit with the panicked look. You're the one who brought kids up."

She was. She had. *Sounds like the sort of thing a man would do for the mother of his children.*

So, did she…want to be the mother of his children?

Though the grin remained fixed on Roman's lips, his thumbs had gone still on her wrists. She looked into his eyes, those brook blue eyes that asked the question in earnest even as he said, "Forget it."

She could see he wanted to know the answer to that question, even as he released her wrists and climbed to his feet. He was too much a family man not to want—to need to know.

Most of all, Roman deserved to know her

answer.

He finished fastening his pants and turned toward the hall, muttering, "The Fire Marshal is waiting."

"What if our daughter wanted to be an architect when she grew up?" she called after him.

He stopped, faced her, his head canted to one side as though he wasn't sure he'd heard her right. "*Our* daughter?"

"Or a doctor, lawyer...mud wrestler?"

A grin tugged at his lips. "I'd expect nothing less of any daughter of yours, Princess."

"And sons, of course," she went on, "would have to have their father's blue eyes."

He advanced on her and took her in his arms. "Son*s*, as in plural?" he said softly. "You don't want to stop at just one of each?"

"I thought you wanted a big family, St. John."

"I do. But I didn't know what you wanted."

"Shut up and kiss me, St. John, before I change my mind."

He pulled her close and kissed her. He kissed her long and hard and deep. And when he finished kissing her, he hugged her close and whispered in her ear, "A mud wrestler?"

Tess levered herself back in his arms and gave him a mock serious look, "If a daughter of mine can't be a mud wrestler if she wants, it's a deal breaker."

He threw his head back and laughed. "Princess, if any daughter of ours wants to be a mud wrestler, I'll get her the finest grit mud to be had in the state of Michigan."

Then he kissed her again, a sweet parting peck on the lips. "I'll go occupy our Fire Marshal while you get yourself straightened up."

Not wanting to be apart from him, she tugged the

hem of the t-shirt down over her hips and said, "There. I'm straightened up."

He rubbed her chin with the pad of his thumb. "Make that cleaned up, too. Much as I find your theatrical make-up adorable—"

"Theatrical make-up?" Her hands flew to her face. "Why didn't you tell me sooner?"

"What, and ruin a great spontaneous moment?" he asked, tapping her on the tip of her nose with a bent knuckle.

She swiped his hand away and wrinkled her nose at him. "Go entertain the Fire Marshal."

#

In the bathroom, Tess looked at herself in the mirror and laughed. There'd been a time she wouldn't have been able to laugh at herself in such a state. But Roman made her feel good about everything, even a soot smudged nose and chin.

She dampened a washcloth and began scrubbing her face. She wanted to make Roman feel good in return. No more hiding behind the shrew. What a fool she'd been.

Been? Or was?

She stopped scrubbing and stared at herself in the mirror above the vanity, watching her grin fade away. Was she being a fool? Had she fallen into the trap of love? Is that why she'd tested Roman's idea of kids as she had?

She dropped the washcloth and looked herself in her mirrored eye. The mere mention of children should have sent her screaming.

Wrong, said the brown eyes looking back at her. *You've always liked kids.*

"Other people's."

Explain that feeling you get in the pit of your

stomach whenever you hold a baby.

"But I want a career."

You can have a career and babies.

"But, to get married is to prove my father right."

A woman doesn't have to marry to have babies.

True. She didn't have to marry. But Roman would never settle for fathering a child without being married to said child's mother. Not that diehard family man.

And you? asked the brown eyes in the mirror.

Until she'd finally gotten the message about the extent of her father's antiquated chauvinism, marriage and children had been part of her life's equation. Her fingers curled into the hem of her t-shirt, the t-shirt Roman had given her to wear the first night she'd invaded his home. She'd clung to Roman's shirt as a way to be close to him.

Roman, whom she'd trusted enough to confess her deepest, darkest fears. Roman, to whom she'd made love, and he to her. Roman, with whom she'd discussed children, that ultimate element that would bind them forever together...because she did want to have his children.

And to spite her father, she was considering denying herself the love of her life? Was she nuts?

#

Tess raced up the attic stairs. She could hear the Fire Marshal talking, but she wasn't listening to what he was saying. She had one thing and only one thing on her mind. Find Roman and tell him she loved him.

Her head cleared the stairwell. She could see Roman's back. The Fire Marshal was facing him and both had their heads bowed as though they looked at something between them.

She cleared the last step and Roman turned

toward her, concern creasing his brow for an instant before a smile smoothed it away. It wasn't quite as bright or as broad a smile as he'd left her with in the bedroom. She wanted to make that smile bright again. She wanted Roman to take her in his arms and kiss her senseless. She headed toward him.

"I take it you're the homeowner," the Fire Marshal said, reminding her he was there.

She couldn't help but smile at his Cheshire cat grin as she sidled up beside Roman. When Roman didn't automatically sling an arm around her, she peered up at him. His smile had turned sad and he lowered his eyes toward the object at the Fire Marshal's feet.

"That's our culprit," he said. "Our fire starter."

Tess looked at the melted glob of orange rubber that vaguely resembled a heavy-duty electrical cord. Her heart skipped a beat. Her gaze traveled up from the glob to the outlet into which it was still plugged then jumped to the black air conditioner cord still linked with the orange extension cord.

"It can't be," she said on a thin breath.

"Don't let the unscathed ends fool you," the Fire Marshal said, toeing the orange glob at their feet. "This is the culprit."

She gaped at the Fire Marshal and stammered, "B-but it's a heavy-duty cord."

"Like I was explaining to your contractor here, even cords rated for heavy-duty use get hot when they draw maximum wattage for an extended period of time. When a cord is coiled up like this one is there's no way for the heat to dissipate."

Tess stared at the cord that looked like something out of a Salvador Dali painting, her toes and fingers suddenly numb.

"We'll check the cord out back at the lab," the Fire Marshal said. "But I've had fires start like this more often than you might think." He gathered up the rest of his test samples, commented that the burn pattern didn't indicate anything out of the ordinary, and said she was free to access her attic then left.

Free? She wasn't free to do anything, not now that she'd seen exactly which cord had caused the fire. Cousin Raymond may have plugged that cord into the air conditioning unit the morning of the fire to cool himself while he labored beneath the eaves to cut and cap an old vent. But she was the one who'd switched the air conditioner back on when she'd come up to the attic to pick through Aunt Honey's storage boxes. She'd been the one who'd left it running all day, overheating the electrical cord...and starting the fire.

Now was not the time to tell Roman she loved him.

But it was the right time to tell him she was at fault for her own fire. "Roman—"

He cut her off with a light kiss. "I need to get back to the job site." Then he kissed her again, a little longer, a little deeper, his lips parting from hers reluctantly and he murmured, "We'll continue this later at home."

It was so tempting to let him go. To put off telling him what was sure to...

Sure to what? Bring on a repeat performance of his pink underwear reaction? Sure to turn him into the raving male chauvinist her father was?

Roman's footsteps echoed up from the stairwell.
Stop him. Tell him now.

She turned, poised to go after him. But her feet seemed stuck in the ash of Aunt Honey's attic. She was normally a woman of action. Why wasn't she running after Roman?

Because, one hint he was anything like her father and she'd be gone before Roman could utter the first syllable of Princess.

There it was. The reason she, woman of action, stood rooted to the sooty floor of a burned out attic rather than facing up to a problem of her own making. She didn't want to find out Roman was like her father.

She hugged her arms across her stomach, an ache the size of the Sears Tower pressing down on her chest. Roman had every right to know it wasn't his fault her assets had gone up in flames. That it was *her* fault he'd spent even one moment worrying about being sued. Her fault he'd been forced to let her invade his home…his life. Sooner or later, she was going to have to tell him.

But, how to tell him.

Honey Buns, don't get mad. I burned up my own attic.

Hey, Roman. Here's something you're going to get a laugh out of.

Look here, St. John. Nobody's perfect.

But plaintive wasn't her style. She didn't feel funny. And she had no business being snippy, especially with Roman.

Straight forward. That was the way to be with him…just like he'd always been with her.

Stop delaying, commanded the little voice in her head. *Go after him and tell him. Now.*

She bounded down the attic steps. He'd reached his truck by the time she hit the front porch.

"Roman," she called.

He turned, the smile on his face wide as a Chicago expressway, and called back at her, "Can't get enough of me today, huh, Princess?"

The toe of her tennis shoe caught in the overgrown lawn as she sprinted across the yard and she almost stumbled. If he went ballistic over what she had to tell him, she'd never get enough of him because she couldn't—wouldn't abide any man dressing her down like a child.

Her heart pounded in her chest. She'd never been so scared in her life, including the night on the lake when she'd nearly drowned. But never before had she so much to lose.

She skidded to a halt just beyond his reach. She didn't dare chance his touch or she might lose her nerve. And, how Roman handled this kind of news was something better learned sooner rather than later. He glanced at the space she left between them and his grin faded.

"If this about my insurance coverage, I've already called the company."

"It's not about your insurance. At least not in the way you're expecting."

His eyes narrowed. "What do you mean, not in the way I'm expecting?"

"I mean you don't have to involve your insurance company."

He blinked, confusion knotting his brow. "I don't understand."

She drew a deep breath. "It wasn't Raymond's fault that cord over-heated."

The lines in Roman's brow curved a less confused more perturbed expression. "If my doltish cousin wasn't such a wimp, he wouldn't have needed air-conditioning for an hour's work under the eaves."

"He shut it off."

"It wouldn't have over-heated if he'd shut it off."

"No. It wouldn't have."

The corners of Roman's mouth pulled downward. "Tess, what are you trying to tell me?"

"I went up in the attic after Raymond left. I turned the air-conditioner on…and forgot to shut it off when I left that day for my run."

He blinked. He looked up at the house, stared at it as though seeing it for the first time. He continued to stare for what seemed an eternity. She held her breath, until…

"So you have nothing to sue me over? And my insurance isn't going to have to shell out big bucks to repair your house? My insurance rates won't go up?"

"That's a good way to look at it," she said.

His gaze dropped to her. He wasn't smiling. Tess' heart tripped against her ribs.

"I'm sorry, Roman. I'm sorry I invaded your home and your life. I'm sorry I inconvenienced you. I'm sorry for every moment of misery I caused you."

In one long stride, he had her in his arms and was swinging her in a circle. Tess clung to him for dear life, all but shrieking, "Aren't you angry with me?"

He set her down between him and his truck, his fingers lingering on her waist reassuring. "I'm relieved, Princess."

"Relieved. That's good."

But, if it was so good, why did she still feel like the ground could drop out from under her at any moment? Why wasn't she sinking into the delicious play of his fingers on her back?

"And you forgive me for being such a—" She looked him in the eye as she finished with the word "—shrew?"

He backed her into the side of the truck, murmuring, "When did I ever call you a shrew?"

"The first night I spent in your house."

"I never called you a shrew." He leaned into her, all his right places lined up with all hers.

"You implied it," she said, still waiting for that proverbial second shoe to drop.

He kissed her neck, humming, "Implied?"

"You were reading *Taming of the Shrew.*" She gulped between passion-induced pants, still trying to see the danger but wanting so much to surrender to the moment.

His chuckle buzzed against her throat. "Figured that one out, did you?"

#

Maybe it was the new state of her financial obligations that put a damper on her mood after Roman drove off whistling a happy tune. Being the owner of a burned out hulk of a house that had been vastly under-insured could turn anyone's mindset to gloom and doom, she'd bemoaned as she drove back to Roman's.

But she was in love, she silently argued as she sat at his desk re-examining the costs to make The Castle whole again now that the expense was hers. Shouldn't love be enough to make any woman happy?

"Any fool of a woman," she muttered, tallying how many two by fours and sheets of plywood it was going to take to patch the hole in the roof. She'd already gone the fool for love route with her father's favorite candidate for son-in-law.

Was that what bothered her? She feared she might have once again fallen into the trap of blinded by love?

Except she hadn't been in love with Harry. She'd been in… What? Joint frustration? Females didn't get ahead at her father's architectural firm and Harry's talents didn't quite live up to his career plans.

She hadn't been blinded by anything. She'd been obsessed by her need for her father's recognition, and Harry's glib promise of a partnership had seemed the answer to that need. Unfortunately for her, Harry had planned on her being the silent partner who provided the talent while he claimed the glory.

Tess slumped back in Roman's office chair. Hashing out old mistakes was not helping her figure out how to save her first solo project from financial ruin. Just what were her options?

Aunt Honey would help her.

But she didn't want to turn to Aunt Honey again. Aunt Honey had helped her enough on this project just by letting her buy The Castle out from under Roman. Besides, she was still incommunicado on some mountain top. So, what other options did she have?

Her father?

When Hell froze over.

Her mother?

Tess grunted. The last financial decision her mother had made was to buy Daddy into the architectural firm where he worked...which he ultimately took over...as he had every penny of Mommy's inheritance.

Except for the trust fund she'd set aside for her future children, a trust containing a marriage clause for any daughters born. She could thank her father for talking her mother into that constraining marriage clause.

A thought hit her like an electrical shock, straightening her from the back of the chair. She couldn't get her hands on her trust until she married. But her sisters were married. Maybe one of them would help.

As quick as hope had flamed, it died. Sister one had handed over the assets of her trust to her investment manager hubby the minute that gold ring had been slipped onto her finger. Dutiful daughter number two had the sense to convert her trust to trusts for her future children. A better option but one that still made any chance of a loan beyond Tess' reach.

With a sigh, Tess sank back into the chair. What to do? With her credit stretched as far as it could go, no bank was going to give her another loan. Another credit card? Given the interest rates, she could forget any profit. Far more likely, she'd be left deep in debt. No success to show to her father.

She pondered the pros and cons of marrying to get her trust fund. There were a lot of pros given the groom in question was Roman. But, what did she really know about him?

Fabulous lover.

Honorable man.

Reliable.

Hard worker.

Family man.

A family man who'd likely turn The Castle into one giant nursery if given the chance. Is this how her father had trapped her mother? Presenting all his good traits during the courtship, not revealing his real self until after the wedding? Could she end up in the same trap—a trap where the husband takes control of the wife's inheritance and adds marriage clauses to your daughters' trust funds?

Besides, marry and her father would declare she'd needed her trust fund to bail her out. So much for proving her abilities as an independent architect and businesswoman to her father.

Tess scowled. How did her father wind up such a

chauvinist with a sister like Honey?

The familiar rumble of Roman's truck pulling into the drive rolled through the house and up her legs. Her heart gave a little lurch. It would be so easy to marry Roman. Thank goodness she had more of Aunt Honey's sense than her mother's. Honey loved her men but handled her own money.

Tess tapped the tip of her pencil against the sheet of paper on the desk on which she'd being figuring repair expenses. Her gaze snagged on the stack of unpaid bills piled beside the list. Bills for the water extraction company, ionizing the air at The Castle, the cleaners who laundered the smoke out of *her* drapes, *her* linens, and *her* clothes and on and on. Roman had taken responsibility for all those expenses because he'd thought the fire was his fault. Now they were her responsibility. Only one option remained if she wanted to avoid bankruptcy and retain her pride.

Downstairs, the front door opened and closed. Desire pinched at Tess' stomach. At least she hoped she had more of Honey's sense.

She could cut her losses and sell the house even if it meant a loss and start over with another project. Now all she needed was someone willing to buy a formerly waterlogged Victorian mansion with a sooty attic.

Roman came up behind her, placed his hands on her shoulders, and kissed the back of her neck. "What are you doing?"

"Figuring out how to keep from going bankrupt on my first project. Know anyone who wants to buy a big old house with a giant hole in its roof?"

His fingers flexed against her shoulders. "Yeah, I do."

She wheeled the chair around so quickly that

they nearly knocked heads. "You know someone willing to pay good money for a half burned out, wreck of a house?"

He smiled crookedly down at her. "Yeah."

"Who is this sucker and point me in his direction."

Roman gripped the arms of the chair and put his face close to hers. "You're already pointed in his direction, and he's not a sucker."

Even though she knew who he was talking about, she stared into his eyes a full ten seconds before speaking the obvious, and still it came out as a question. "You?"

"I've always wanted The Castle. You know that, Tess."

She shook her head in disbelief. "But, it's a wreck."

"It's not as bad as it seems, especially for a contractor with the resources to repair it."

If this was the answer to her prayers, why wasn't she jumping up and down with joy?

For the same reason she wasn't jumping into marriage so she could get her hands on her trust fund.

"You're bailing me out," she said.

"I'm offering to buy The Castle at salvage price. I get a bargain and you don't lose your shirt on the deal. If that's bailing you out, so what?"

"So this is strictly a business proposition?" she quizzed cautiously.

"That would be one way of putting it," he allowed. "But, there is another option, another proposal I'd like you to consider."

He took her hands in his and went down on one knee. "Marry me, Tess."

Hope, desire, and happiness exploded through

her. Why then, did she hesitate to answer?

A jumble of thoughts careened around inside her skull. Marry the man she loved…and give up her independence. Get access to her trust fund…and lose her integrity. She couldn't cook and was a disaster at laundry. Why on earth would Roman St. John want to marry her?

Did it have something to do with the business proposition he'd first offered her? Harry had had prefaced his marriage proposal with business, too. Though he hadn't offered both propositions in the same conversation—and hadn't been anywhere near as straight forward with either proposal. But the result would be the same. Her blood began to boil.

"I suppose you already have the ring," she managed in a level voice.

"It hasn't been sized yet," he responded enthusiastically and reached into his shirt pocket.

"That sure I'd say yes, huh?"

He paused without opening the little blue velvet box he held in his hand, his enthusiasm fading. "Tess, we've had some serious conversation lately. We talked about kids today. That's the sort of thing that makes a man think—"

"That he's found his June Cleaver?"

Frown lines furrowed his brow. "It sounded like we wanted the same things."

"Like babies?"

"Yeah."

"Like filling The Castle with them?"

"Yes."

"Maybe a big playroom in the attic?"

"Yesss," he answered warily.

"And of course that walk-in closet goes back to being a nursery."

He narrowed his eyes as though he was beginning to get her message. "We can compromise—"

She stood, the chair rolling back from her. "I'm not some damsel in need of rescuing, St. John."

He jerked to his feet. "I'm not trying to rescue—"

"I'll take option one. The business deal."

"Dammit, Tess, what are you so angry about?"

She jabbed her chin at him. "I'm angry about men controlling my life."

"I'm not trying to control—"

"The hell you're not! You just told me you want to turn The Castle into one giant nursery."

"I thought you wanted the same thing."

"I bought The Castle as an investment, to remodel and sell. Nowhere in your little proposition did you provide for my plans for the house."

"Okay, so I jumped the gun. I thought—"

"All the baby talk automatically meant I was willing to subjugate myself to you?"

"No. That's not—"

"You had it all planned out. You get the girl, the kids, and the house all in one neat deal."

"I thought we wanted the same things," he murmured, standing there in front on her, his arms hanging at his sides, the little velvet box dangling between his fingers. She could almost feel sorry for him. But, damn it, she was fighting for her independence here. And independence meant life to her.

"You want The Castle that bad, St. John? It's yours, at salvage price of course. Put all the nurseries in it you want."

"Tess," he pleaded.

She skirted him for the doorway. "Have the

papers drawn up and sent to me at my Chicago address. That's where I'll be."

"You can't mean that, Tess."

"More than anything," she said from the doorway. "And don't even try to come after me."

CHAPTER THIRTEEN

Tess sipped at her morning latte as she watched the pedestrians hurrying past her sidewalk café table. In the past week, she'd gone to a play, a blues club, and a comedy club. She'd visited Navy Pier, The Museum of Natural Art, and the Shedd Aquarium. She'd eaten deep-dish pizza from her favorite Chicago pizzeria, Italian ice at a neighborhood ethnic fair, and ballpark franks in the cheap seats at a Cubs game. She'd done all her favorite things. But none had cheered her up.

Why? Why hadn't the fireworks off Navy Pier made her "ooh" and "aah?" Why had the breakers rolling in off Lake Michigan made her feel melancholy? Why, when she'd tossed coins into Buckingham Fountain, hadn't she been able to put her wish into words?

She knew why.

No amount of wishes could guarantee Roman wasn't just like her father or former fiancé. Besides, Roman was a country boy and she a city gal. He wanted a housewife. She wanted a career.

She was in Chicago and he hadn't come after her.

She scowled into her latte. What did she expect? Whenever she fingered the car keys on her condo kitchen counter and thought of roads lined with trees instead of concrete streets shadowed by skyscrapers, she'd called her sisters and her mother for a reminder of what marriage did to a woman. A reminder why the dream of a big, old house humming with activity wasn't hers. A reminder why she denied herself the man for whom her heart still yearned.

A couple lovers strolled past her sidewalk table, fingers entwined and heads together. At a neighboring table, two little girls giggled over oatmeal raisin cookies and cocoa while their mother and father beamed at them. At the street corner, an elderly man held up a hand to the oncoming traffic as he helped his wife onto the curb, who hadn't quite finished crossing before the light had changed.

Tess couldn't help but wonder if she was doomed to forever be no more than an observer of people in love? To be a stranger sitting at a sidewalk café sipping lattes and watching old women smile at their life mates for helping them cross streets. How that smile lit up the old woman's face. How the old man's face softened as he looked into his wife's.

Who would help her cross the street when she was old? Who would be there for her to smile at…and to smile back at her?

No one, as long as marriage and loss of independence went hand in hand. That's why she'd played the shrew with Roman. That's why she'd refused his *proposal* even though she loved him. That's why she was clinging to her need to control her own life.

The old couple trundled off down the street arm in arm. Maybe it was worth giving up a little control to have that.

"Tess Abbot," intoned a familiar voice. "I heard you were back in town."

She raised her chin toward the man standing beside her table in a dark gray suit, crisp white shirt, and power tie, the man who'd shown her just how dangerous it could be to relinquish control.

"Hello, Harry," she leveled at her ex-fiancé.

He smiled his dazzle 'em-with-bull smile. "You're looking good, Tess."

She thought about the amount of make-up she'd had to apply to cover the circles under her eyes sleepless nights had caused. "What do you want, Harry?"

He grunted through his fixed smile. "Now why would you assume I want something?"

"You never liked this café. This corner is out of your way. And everything you ever did with and for me, you did because you wanted something."

He dipped his chin, his smile tightening at its corners. "Cynicism does not become you, Doll."

"I'm not your Doll, Harry. What do you want?"

"You're going to make me get right to the point, aren't you?"

"If you don't get to the point soon, Harry, you're going to be talking to an empty chair because I have no interest in playing your games ever again." She started to get up.

He put a hand on the back of her chair and leaned over her. "Okay. Here's the deal. Remember that little project you helped me with?"

"You mean the low income housing design I developed for which you took the credit?" she shot back, refusing to shrink from him.

His lips tightened over a solicitous smile. "We're not going to rehash that now, are we?"

She arched an eyebrow at him. "You're the one who brought it up."

He sighed and eased back from her. "I couldn't very well not bring it up when I'm here to offer you a chance to get back in on that project."

She studied her ex-fiancé, noting the intensity

with which he watched her, how he held his breath, and the white knuckles of the hand he seemingly draped casually over the back of her chair. "You're in trouble with the design, aren't you?"

He snorted as though she'd just said the most absurd thing, but the pressure of his fingers telegraphed agreement through the metal frame of the chair. "I'm offering you a chance to get back on board. That's all."

"In that case, no thank you." She pushed her chair back from the table and rose, making him release the chair.

"B-but—"

He seemed to catch himself before he said more. But the damage had been done because Harry never sputtered.

She looked him in the eye. She could just walk away. She knew he was in trouble. But she wanted him to admit it.

"You stole a perfectly good design from me, Harry. What could you have possibly done to screw it up?"

He smiled indulgently at her. "We've been all through this, Tess. You created that design on company time. It belongs to the firm. Nobody stole it from you."

"Swell." She snatched the disposable coffee cup off the table and headed toward the trash receptacle. "Then take your problems to the firm that owns my design. Take your problems to my father."

"I already did," he rushed out, following her, not sounding at all smug now. "We're both in trouble with it."

She turned to him. "How *can* you be? That was a simple plan."

He stuffed his hands in his trouser pockets, rocked back on his heels, and shrugged. "You know the government, always demanding modifications."

"So make them."

He looked down at the toes of his wingtip shoes then peered up at her. It was his contrite boyish look. He'd used it on her before when she'd caught him in the small manipulations, the ones she'd let slide because she knew what it was like to not quite measure up.

"Everything we've tried has been rejected," he said, "and we're running out of time."

A bark of laughter escaped Tess. "Then you're screwed, Harry."

She started off down the sidewalk.

"This doesn't affect just me," he called after her. "It's costing your father big time."

She considered shouting back that he and her father could both go jump in Lake Michigan. But, here was her chance to get what she wanted from her father. Recognition as an architect. She'd be a fool to pass it up.

There was something else she sensed she was being a fool about. But, at the moment she couldn't quite put her finger on what it was.

\#

It was nearly dark by the time Tess crossed the skyway from the Abbot offices to the parking ramp. It was as close to seeing daylight as she'd gotten in the past five days. But she'd recaptured the integrity of the design that had initially won the government contract for her father's firm while making the necessary cost cuts, and she'd done it all under deadline.

The client still had to approve the final design,

but she was confident they would. Most importantly, she was done with it.

Done with the job. Done with Harry. Done with her father...at least on a professional level.

Any latent thoughts she might have had about rejoining her father's firm had vanished after five life-blood sucking days working with him. He'd actually been condescending to her about her coming to her senses and returning home. So much for gaining his approval. At least she'd had the satisfaction of seeing the shocked look on his face when she'd told him she'd mail him her consulting bill.

She now knew beyond a doubt she did not need her father's approval; and she'd found that realization liberating.

She steered her car out of the company parking garage with a relieved lightness. Something else she'd learned in the past five days. She definitely wanted more out of life than to be an architect. She loved the work—the creating, was passionate about it. But even the most creative work in the world couldn't love you back. Not in the way a life-partner could.

She thought of the old couple she had seen the previous week crossing the street together. They'd looked as if they'd spent a lifetime together loving one another. She wanted that, all of that.

The Chicago skyline glided by, the setting sun blazing in the high-rise windows. She loved the city. But she'd come to realize it wasn't enough for her, not without someone with whom to share her life. And she knew exactly who she wanted as her life mate.

What a fool she'd been. A silly, shrewish fool. Roman was nothing like Harry or her father. A week of those two and she'd seen the difference between controlling and supportive. Harry and her father wanted to take control because they believed she, a woman, incapable. Roman took charge because he was decisive. Her father and Harry had tried to control her. Roman supported her.

Tess smiled. She would go to Roman and apologize for walking away from him—for turning back into the shrew. That last part should bring a smile to his lips. She could almost feel them slanting across hers, could almost feel his arms slipping around her, his hand cradling her head as he kissed her—and forgave her for her own stupidity.

She pulled up in front of her condo building and exited her car, turning it over to the valet. A stiff breeze cut under her suit jacket like a premonition and she shivered. What if Roman wouldn't forgive her? What if he'd come to his senses and realized she wasn't the woman he wanted? She wasn't close to being the domestic goddess he deserved. What would she do then?

"Wish him well and let him go to find the woman he deserves," she murmured as she strode toward the building's double doors.

But that was not going to happen. No way. No how. Roman St. John loved her and she loved him. She was going to fight for him.

End of story.

At least it would be the end of the story once she got back to Pine Mountain and climbed a certain contractor's six-foot plus frame.

The doors swung open before her and she nearly skipped into the condo's lobby. "Thank you, Carlton," she sang to the security guard behind the circular desk who monitored who got through those double doors and who didn't. "How'd your Libby's wrestling match go?"

"She won against a boy who was top in his weight division last year."

She leaned over the desk, caught Carlton by the tie, tugged him close, and gave the guard a kiss on the cheek.

"What's that for?" he asked through a sheepish grin.

"For being a great father."

She practically pirouetted toward the elevators, but Carlton stopped her with, "Oh, Miss Abbott. There's a gentleman waiting to see you."

She turned halfway back to the guard who nodded toward the seating area on the far side of the main entrance. She turned further and saw him rise from one of the leather club chairs. Roman St. John…in khaki chinos and a blue knit polo shirt the same amazing hue as his eyes.

Her heart skipped a beat. Then surged into an 'I'll do anything if you'll forgive me' cadence as he approached. But, before she could utter a single syllable, he held out a thick, manila envelope.

"I brought you the contract for The Castle."

The sales papers. That's why he was here. Not for her. For The Castle. He'd figured out he deserved better than a shrew who couldn't cook or wash clothes.

"You could have messengered them," she said more sharply than she intended.

He had stopped barely within reach, the distance like a chasm between them. "And which Pine Mountain messenger service would you have had me use?"

She wanted to rewind the past ten seconds. Wanted to replay what she'd said and how she'd said it. She wanted to take time to analyze the guarded look in his eyes. But she couldn't help but feel she'd run out of time and she couldn't take back the last few seconds any more than she could change the past several weeks.

Maybe this was the way he wanted it—needed it to be. Maybe, in her heart, she too knew this was how it should be. Hadn't she reverted to the shrew when she'd walked out on him…as she had every other time she'd needed to push him away? Maybe this time he needed her to push him away because sometimes parting on friendly terms was just too painful.

She should sign the papers here in the lobby so he could get back to the life he deserved…and she could go upstairs to her high-rise condo alone and cry her way through a chocolate fudge brownie. But she didn't have any brownies.

She nodded toward the elevators. "Let's do this upstairs."

#

He'd given her time and space. He'd thought that's all she needed. But she hadn't come back to Pine Mountain, hadn't come home. So he'd come to her.

Roman stood staring out the expanse of windows that made up one wall of Tess' condo, the view of the waterfront reflecting the city lights spectacular. Nothing like that in Pine Mountain.

Nothing like her straight out of the pages of *Architects' Digest* condo, either. His heart sank. The place fit her princess style.

Correction. The condo fit the style of the talented architect she was.

She personified the upwardly mobile type in her navy pumps whose heels were just high enough and pin-striped suit-skirt's hem just short enough to say professional yet remind him how sinfully good those legs could feel wrapped around his hips. The minute he'd seen her, he'd wanted to scoop her up in his arms and kiss her silly. He'd wanted to tell her he loved her and beg her to give them another chance. But, she'd looked so happy when she'd walked into the condo lobby that he'd realized he had no right to ask her to leave all this. Not if this was what made her happy.

So he'd given her a sale's contract instead of a kiss.

He turned from the windows—faced where she sat reading through the contract on a white couch. Not exactly kid friendly furniture.

Tess' world. So she'd hit it off with his nephew, cooed at her neighbors baby, and gone all maternal over an injured dog. Maybe she even wanted kids.

Of course she wanted kids. With me, even. She'd talked about *our* kids—about a mud wrestling daughter. But that didn't mean she wanted to raise them in a burg of a town. And here he'd gone and given her enough time to figure that out.

Better to figure it out sooner than later, echoed the voice of reason between his ears. Not that sound reasoning made him feel any better.

He should leave while he still could with some dignity. He should leave before his feelings overrode his good sense and he begged her to come back to Pine Mountain—leave her at peace in the city where she belonged.

But, he hadn't driven three hundred miles just to walk away without fight, ego be damned. Time to lay all his cards on the table.

"What do I need to do to convince you to give us another chance, Tess? Rebuild my contracting business here in Chicago?"

The air went out of Tess as though she'd been punched in the stomach. He hadn't written her off, and she all but gasped, "You'd move your business for me?"

"For us."

All the doubts, hopes, and questions that'd been tumbling through her brain as she'd pretended to read the contract vanished. "But you've worked hard to build your business, your reputation in Pine Mountain."

"I can easily rebuild the business here. My references won't disappear and, I assume, I'd have your endorsement."

"Of course, but The Castle…"

"You haven't signed the papers yet. We could finish the renovation and sell it like you planned."

"But, you wanted to raise a family in a small town."

His eyes narrowed at her. "You trying to talk me out of moving to Chicago, Princess? Because if you've moved on, just tell me and we can end this right now."

She rose from the couch, the contract slipping from her fingers. "No. I… It's just… In the lobby you were all business when you handed me the contract. I thought it meant you'd moved on."

"You looked so happy when you entered the lobby…" He shook his head. "In that moment, I knew I could never take from you anything that makes you that happy."

She took a step toward him, her heart hammering. "I was happy because I had an incredibly good day. A great week, in fact."

He eyed her narrowly. "What happened this past week that made you so happy?"

"Remember the project my ex-fiancé stole from me that won my father a big contract?"

"Yeah."

"Seems the government wanted some modifications and Harry and my father couldn't figure out how to make them and still keep the project profitable."

The tension in his posture gave and a ghost of a smile tugged at the corner of his mouth. "Enter Tess Abbott, girl architect to the rescue."

Her heart skipped a beat and she chanced a quippy, "I'll overlook that girl reference this once because I did indeed rescue the project."

"Do you feel vindicated?" he asked, taking a step toward her, further narrowing the space between them.

"Very much so," she said, her heart pounding a far more hopeful rhythm. "Especially after telling my father I'd mail him my consulting bill."

He closed the space between them. "Good for you."

She looked up into his face, her heart pounding so hard surely he had to hear it. "Best of all, I no longer feel the need to prove anything to him."

"Even better." He cupped her cheek. "And now that we've determined we both suffered a near fatal moment of misunderstanding in the lobby, does my offer to relocate here provide a compromise we both can live with?"

She wanted to settle into the comfort of his hand. But she needed to know whatever he proposed wouldn't turn into resentment. She looked him deep in the eye. "I can't take away from you what makes you happy, either, Roman."

His fingers stilled on the hinge of her jaw, the

lobe of her ear. "I've lived all over the world, Tess, mostly in cities. One of the best lessons my mother taught me was home is where you make it. I won't be unhappy."

"Even though you wanted to raise a family in a small town?"

"Kids grow up fine in cities. I'm a good example of that, no?"

She smiled up at him. "Yes."

"Then we've got a deal?"

She draped her hands over his shoulders and threaded her fingers behind his neck. "Not quite."

He arched back against her hold. "What do you mean, not quite?"

"We don't need the city. We already have a home in a quiet, safe little town. A big home with wonderful neighbors."

He eyed her skeptically. "But you love the city."

"Yes, I do. And we can always visit. But a city can't love me back the way you can." She leaned in, kissing him just below the ear and murmuring, "So, are we ready to start a life together in a castle of a house surrounded by a neighborhood full of friends?"

He pressed his lips to her temple. "Are you sure. Tess?"

She settled her head against his shoulder. "Yes, I'm sure. Are you sure you want to marry a woman who's a domestic disaster?"

His arms tightened around her. "There's not a doubt in my mind you're the woman for me."

"I'll turn our children's underwear pink."

He kissed one corner of her mouth. "It'll teach the boys to be tough."

"You're neat and I'm messy."

He kissed the other corner of her mouth. "If you

think you're messy, wait till we have kids."

"I'll burn their food."

She felt his smile stretch against her ear lobe as he whispered, "They won't know the difference. Kids think whatever they grow up with is normal. Besides—" he nipped her earlobe. "—who's to say you have to do all the cooking?"

She pulled back from him and looked up into his face. "They'll know the difference when they compare my cooking to yours."

He grinned. "They'll grow up nostalgic about it, then. Ever since those hamburgers you cooked, I know I've found myself getting misty-eyed over the aroma of singed food."

She cuffed him on the shoulder. "Careful there. Just because I love you doesn't mean you've got a deal."

He grinned. "You love me."

"Yeah. And you love me," she retorted. "Now, how are we going to manage this partnership?"

"Are these negotiations going to take all night?" he asked, slipping a hand between them and popping free the top button of her suit jacket.

She slid hand down over his backside, purring, "Maybe."

His grin stretched and button two popped free. Desire pinched at Tess' stomach. But she sobered.

"Kids aren't anything to mess around with. How can you be sure I'll be a good parent?"

"Because you have the right parenting instincts where it counts." he said, his hot fingers pressing the cool, silk camisole under her jacket into the valley between her breasts. "You'll be better than good. You are going to be great."

She sighed. "You deserve a woman who's a

domestic goddess."

He laughed, his amazing blue gaze meeting hers. "Boring. What I want is the woman I *need*, Tess. A woman who spices up my life—who makes me use my heart more and my head less."

"And I need you, Roman St. John. I need you to tame away my stubborn reactionary ways."

"Just promise me one thing, Princess," he murmured as he lowered his mouth toward hers.

"Anything."

"Don't get too tame on me."

The End

Excerpt from FINDING HOME
St. John Sibling Series, Book 2
By Barbara Raffin

"That woman's not fit to raise my grandson!" The old man slammed his palm down on the mahogany desk behind which he stood.

Sam Ryan shifted in the ancient leather chair on the one-who'd-been-summoned side of the desk. So much for pointing out the old man's son had wed *that* woman.

"As for Michael's good judgment," the old man growled, bracing both hands against the broad desktop and leaning toward him.

And strike two.

"She seduced him. Trapped him into marriage."

If the old man was implying she'd gotten pregnant to force a proposal, then the pregnancy would have been a record at thirteen months post wedding.

Not that Sam was going to make the mistake of pointing out yet another flaw in the old man's reasoning. He'd been properly reminded how futile it was to argue with Stuart Carrington. Twenty-five years since he'd first sat in this chair under the scrutiny of an uncle who had it within his power to decide his future and he still felt every bit the six year old boy he'd been then.

Which brought Sam to the question that had nagged him ever since his uncle had summoned him back from the banished lands abroad. Why welcome the family black sheep back into the fold now? It couldn't be to replace Mickey. Hell, Mickey had died over two years ago. If the old man wanted a replacement son, he'd have called him home sooner.

Not that Sam wanted to replace Mickey...not that he could. Mickey had been the big brother he'd wanted—needed, giving him the sense of family his globetrotting mother hadn't and buffering him from his uncle's wrath when he screwed up...which was most of the time. He'd idolized Mickey—loved him. The one thing his uncle ne surrogate father and he had in common. They both loved Michael.

No, Stuart Carrington would never replace his son with his sister's mongrel whelp. But a grandson...

Sam sighed in resignation, having known deep down all along the reason he'd been summoned. The specifics were what he didn't know. "Why am I here?"

His uncle's flinty eyes narrowed at him. "I need you."

Sam's heart lurched in his chest before his brain could intercept the reflex. To be *needed* by the only father figure he'd ever known fed into the hunger of the lost boy still inside him. He hated it because he knew whatever his uncle asked of him, he would do.

#

So here he was, two hundred plus miles north of Chicago sitting in an empty parking lot under a darkened restaurant sign, the Ducati bike engine rumbling with a throaty purr between his legs. Another perk of doing the old man's bidding, getting the keys to whatever vehicle he wanted from his uncle's collection along with the promise that when he finished the job and headed back to Paris the bike went with him. But, did he love the bike enough to ruin a woman's life? That was one of the questions that had sent him riding aimlessly along country roads rather than sticking to the highway and its direct route to his destination.

Sam peered up at the white-washed farmhouse gilded by a setting sun. Its multi-gabled upper floors cast soft shadows across the scalloped shingles of the inviting wrap around porch. Beneath the overhang, warm yellow light filtered from the curtained windows of the Victorian era farmhouse's first floor. Even the sidewalk was flower lined. Currier and Ives couldn't have painted a more idyllic scene. Hardly the setting he'd expected of a gold-digger.

But appearances could be deceiving. He knew. For all the mischief and decadence of his thirty plus years, for all the running away from his uncle he'd done, all he coveted was family acceptance. Yup, all he had to do was dig up some dirt on a woman who'd never done him any wrong and he'd be back in Stuart's good graces.

He flicked off the bike's engine, dismounted and stepped out from under the free-standing sign that read *The Farmhouse*. Appearances indeed could be deceiving, he thought as he gazed into the warm glow of the windows of a home turned into a restaurant.

With his Ducati-silver and red helmet tucked under his arm, he climbed the broad front steps. A figure moved beyond the first floor curtains, a distinctly female figure. Mickey's widow cleaning up after a day of diners? He hesitated ever so briefly at the top of the porch stairs, doubt still niggling at him. Would Mickey approve of what he was about to do?

He would if it saved his son from a mother who used the boy to gain his trust fund. And Stuart was certain she was holding his grandson as collateral against the inheritance he denied her. Ransom had been the kindest of the words his uncle had used to describe his daughter-in-law's refusal to give the boy up to his care—his very money-advantaged care.

Sam stood there facing the leaded glass panel of the front door—facing his dilemma. Was he really doing this for Mickey's family or for himself? Mickey, after all, had chosen her—married her—fathered a child with her; and Mickey had never been fooled by womanly enchantments.

Then again, perhaps he could do right for both family and self. What harm would there be in visiting Mickey's wife and kid if there was no dirt to dig up? After all, Uncle Stu's army of detectives hadn't ferreted out anything he could use in court. What were the odds he, the family screw-up, would find anything?

And if he did?

Mickey would want his kid protected. The kid was all that mattered.

Still, Sam opened his silver windbreaker with the red Ducati emblem and let in the balmy breath of the summer evening. As if anything could warm him—make him feel less reptilian about introducing himself to his cousin-in-law as a friend.

"Simon Legree had more heart," he muttered and raised his hand to knock on the door.

Yet something stilled his hand. Mickey, who'd raised a child with this woman for two years? Mickey, who'd emailed him pictures of a happy family and written endlessly of his love for them? Was the memory Mickey's way of trying to give him one more chance to do the right thing—the honorable thing? And was the right thing to leave?

Sam began to back away from the door. That's when he heard the clatter of toenails coming fast toward him from the side porch—when the vibration of the heavy footfalls reverberated up his legs from the old floorboards. He turned for the stairs just as the biggest dog he'd ever seen skidded around the porch corner, ears flying, jowls flapping, strings of drool trailing from a fang filled mouth.

He flung his helmet at the black and white blur of a dog coming at him, turned, and threw his body against the front door. But the door didn't budge. The next thing he knew, he was plastered against the leaded glass panel of the door and a pair of massive paws pinned him by the shoulders.

About the Author

An obsessive writer who'd rather write than breathe, Barbara Raffin wrote her first novel at age twelve in retaliation to the lack of female leads in the adventure stories she loved reading. But it was a love of playing with words, exploring the human psyche, and telling stories that kept her writing.

This award-winning author lives on the Michigan-Wisconsin border with her Keeshond dogs Katie and Slippers and her avid outdoorsman husband who has always supported her love affair with reading and writing. Learn more about Barbara Raffin and her books, or contact her through her web site at www.BarbaraRaffin.com